THE LAST SERIAL KILLER

R.G. Crossley

DEDICATION

To the love my life, Rita, who keeps me grounded and who believes in my work. Her love and support means more to me than she will ever know.

ACKNOWLEDGMENTS

Big thank you's must go to my editors, Leigh and Lyn, for their outstanding work on making this story all it can be. Also, many thanks to the folks at Lucky Bat Books, Cindie and Judith, for their support with this project. And last but not least to Jeff Sturgeon for his incredible talent as an artist and being able to encapsulate my story with his wonderful cover. Thanks, Jeff.

INTRODUCTION

This novel had its gestation while on a road trip to the Oregon Coast to attend a workshop taught by my mentors, professional fiction writers, Dean Wesley Smith and Kristine Kathryn Rusch. Driving along Interstate 5 headed for Oregon had become routine and too often we listened to talk stations on the car radio, both the so-called left and right sides of the political spectrum. As a Canadian I have no stake in American politics so I listen to both sides to gain some perspective on the issues of the day as seen through the American lens.

This particular day I passed a sign for an off ramp to Todd Road and an idea struck me. What if in the future there was a right wing radio host named Todd Road, and like many of the talk radio hosts I'd been hearing, he humiliated a frequent guest, a serial killer on death row? Interesting. But what if someone claimed the serial killer was innocent? And what if the serial killer was the last of his kind? More interesting. What if the person proclaiming the killers innocent is from another planet? Now this is very intriguing.

The result of these seemingly diverse ideas resulted in my going on a journey to explore the suspense genre set against a near future backdrop, with a dash of science fiction thrown into the mix. The finished work is different than anything I've ever read, but somehow it works.

I hope you enjoy this suspense filled ride into a possible future with an unlikely hero.

Enjoy.

Russ 2012

The Last Serial Killer

ISBN 978-0-9876701-0-6

Published by:
53rd Street Publishing
Vancouver, B.C. Canada
www.53rdsteetpublishing.com

ONE

"They're coming." The caller's voice in his earpiece was barely above a whisper.

Todd Road's gray eyes scanned the list of names and link numbers on the white computer screen recessed into his work station. The glossy black desk extended from the control board console covered in touch screen buttons and indicators for sound and light levels in KZAP's studio. His heart beat faster when his eyes locked on the caller's name and the origin of the call.

Todd drew in a breath and held it, his chest tightening. It was him. Serial murderer, Mike Sikes was calling his show again. And Elmore Watts said radio was dead back in '22? What the hell did he know? In 2067 talk radio was once again the king of all media. (At least according to Smith and Wesson, his principal sponsor.)

Guy Thompson, the KZAP news director, his boss, was pressuring Todd to get rid of this nut. But nuts were the staple of his show, and Sikes was the craziest and highest-rated nut every listener loved to hate. The ad revenues for the station had tripled in the last six moths since Sikes started calling. But Guy, like many a new bride, was getting cold feet. Depending on a serial murderer for ratings wasn't his idea of good radio.

The more times Mike called, the more Todd found himself agreeing with Guy.

He'd made a vow to himself to only take three more calls, then he'd cut the bastard loose.

"What do you mean, Mike?" he said unenthusiastically.

"The aliens are coming. To Earth. They want to know why." Mike Sikes's voice was surprisingly calm for someone who had just edged over the crazy line. Sikes had finally lost touch with reality, as if he'd ever been in the reality where everyone else lived at all.

Not that Todd knew how crazy was supposed to sound. Many of the callers to his program, 'On the Road with Todd Road – The Conservatives Conservative,' were on the fringe of mainstream society, but he wouldn't call them crazy – exactly. They were patriots. Honest, hard-working Americans, average folks let down by their government. A view he shared.

"Mike, you know my opinions on little green men from other planets."

"I know, Mr. Road, but they've been speaking to me for a long time, and they need my help. That's why they're coming here."

He sounded serious. Todd thought it was time to give the guy a blast, something he'd perfected in his ten years behind the microphone, and get rid of this loony.

"Sure, Mike, there are aliens inside your head talking to you. Just you, no one else in the world, just good 'ol boy, Mike Sikes, serial killer. Sure that sounds plausible." Todd made a circle by the side of his head, which made his producer on the other side of the glass wall separating them, grin and chuckle.

Amy Rickland, a flaxen-haired woman of thirty-five, was a damn good producer. — a fact Todd frequently told the station manager — and she was a staunch conservative, which made her a real find in the world of talk radio.

Being slim and attractive didn't hurt either.

"You can make fun of me all you want," said Mike sounding the not least bit upset at Todd's attempt to humiliate him on national radio. "But I'm telling you, they'll be here in a week's time, and they'll be looking for you."

Todd's gray-streaked eyebrows rose in surprise. "Me? Mike, why would they want to meet a little 'ol radio guy like me?" He winked at Amy, who smiled. She signaled they had to break for the news in thirty seconds.

"You're the only one who knows I'm innocent."

Anger flared in Todd. He'd being saying this to stir up his audience. He never expected Mike to believe he actually supported the sonofabitch bloody killer. "Well, folks that's about all we need to hear from Massacre Mike." He hit the cut off button ending the call. "Time for the news at the top of the hour. We'll be back in ten."

The red, on-air light over the glass wall went dark. He stole a glance at the digital clock on the control board. He had ten minutes, and his bladder was screaming for relief.

Todd pulled the ear-mike from his right ear then rose stiffly from his maroon-colored chair. He stretched his arms over his head, his ample belly straining against the white plastic buttons that ran down his light indigo shirt.

I'm getting old, thought Todd. He ran one bloated hand over his hairless head.

Amy opened the door to the booth. "Hey, boss, you think that guy knows something we don't?"

Todd glanced at her and smiled sardonically, "Never believe everything you hear. Especially in the talk-radio business, my sweet."

Striding through the open door he passed a chuckling Amy and was soon standing over a urinal in the men's room.

Too much coffee again this morning,. When was he going to learn?

Maybe Mike was telling the truth, at least as he knew it. Todd didn't think murderers were crazy — psychotic sure, but they deserved to reap what they sowed. Death was too good from them. Mike may be a loon, but he sure sounded convinced he'd been talking to real aliens. So if Mike wasn't making any of this up, why include Todd?

Todd zipped his fly, reminding himself that he wanted no part of Mike Sikes or his kooky ideas. But since had had helped Mike create the fantasy of his innocence to pump up his ratings, he did feel a certain obligation to let the madness roll on until they stuck the needle in Mike's arm.

"Then it's be good riddance to the stinking garbage," he muttered to himself. He glanced at himself in the mirror. "Some days, Road, I don't like you very much," he said to his reflection.

As he washed his hands, he made up his mind to tell Amy to ban the guy from the show. Guy was right, Mike had been calling long enough. Since Mike was the last of his kind (medical science had seen to that) he'd managed to squeeze out a few perks out of the warden.

Two years on death row must have bent the guy's brain severely out of shape. Didn't matter anyway; another six months and he was going to fry. Well, not exactly fry. It would be more like death by drug overdose, which had been the preferred method of execution for the Department of Corrections for several decades.

Todd pitied Mike's victims far more than their murderer. They had suffered painful, lingering deaths at his hands, Mike wouldn't suffer, but at least he'd be dead. As far as Todd was concerned the system was too lenient with these guys. Maybe he'd discuss that in the next segment.

The heartless monster had inspired whole new discussions around the death penalty, one of Todd's favorite topics. He had hoped to have Mike on the show one more time, just before he was sent to the great beyond. But now Mike was trying to change his carefully crafted agenda and talk about little green men. Todd had already spoken with the program director about scheduling the event his code word for Mike's execution. He smiled at himself in the mirror over the sink. "You're sooo smart, Mr. Road," he said to his reflection.

The smile faded as he gazed at the dark circles under his gray eyes.

"But you look like shit, Road. You gotta get some sleep one of these nights," he murmured. Insomnia was a curse in his family.

He sighed and left the men's room heading back to the booth. Amy greeted him at the door with a stunned look on her face. Her heavy layer of makeup couldn't hide the pale pallor of her skin and the fear in her eyes.

"What's wrong?" he said.

"Guy... from the newsroom called up…" Her voice trailed off to an unintelligible whisper.

Her body trembled.

"What?" Was it a death in her family, was it in his family? Not that he had much of one left. At forty he wasn't married, though he did have a sister, Izzy, who lived in Baltimore with her two kids. He tried to recall Izzy's husband's name, but it eluded him.

Amy looked at him with watery eyes. She was always so controlled and calm about things that seeing her like this shook him to the core.

Placing his meaty hands on her narrow shoulders her held her. She was really trembling, almost as if she'd been in a walk-in freezer like the ones they had in restaurants and couldn't get her temperature back up.

"They're here," she whispered finally from between trembling lips.

"Who's here?" he asked, his guts were twisted by fear struggling to comprehend what he already suspected

The aliens had arrived.

She shook her head. "Mike was right…."

Todd let go of her shoulders and hurried into the newsroom. His show was over for the moment.

Heads turned as he walked in. Guy sat in his office barking orders to his staff from behind his desk. He was frantically typing an e-mail, his fingers pounding the keyboard when Todd entered the noisy room.

The office reeked of stale coffee and donuts, a reporter's primary food groups. The reporters around the room wore ear-links clipped to the rims of their ears as they gazed at their computer screens mesmerized by something on the screen.

Todd walked to the nearest workstation where a reporter he knew only as Mary sat transfixed, staring at the image on her screen.

Todd moved closer to see what was on her screen. His heart rate increased st the sight of a shot obviously from the Hubble V telescope. The object in the center of the screen was a vessel, a space ship, a flying saucer — whatever he called it, it was what every sci-fi fan would instantly recognize as an alien spacecraft.

The ship was long and shaped like a cigar. There wasn't a fiery tail, like in those cheap sci-fi flicks of so long ago, but the object moved across the screen as he watched.

At the bottom right of the screen was the word 'LIVE' and the red letters of the CNN logo beside it.

"This is real," he whispered. Mary nodded, her arms crossed over her red blouse her blond hair golden in the glare of the overhead florescent lights.

Todd broke away and rushed into Guy's office, slamming the door behind him.

The pane of glass in the wood-framed door rattled as it closed.

Guy glared at him. He was completely bald, having shaved-off the fringe that was all that remained of his once brown hair a few years previous. His intense blue eyes were fixed on Todd.

He sat behind a glass-topped desk in a high-backed, brown leather executive chair. On the wall behind him were numerous — too many to count — certificates and holographs of him with some of the country's leading movers and shakers in the radio, political, and movie industries. In all of the pictures Guy wore a wide, toothpaste smile.

Right now though Guy looked none-too-happy.

"Did you know about this?" he asked in his gravely voice.

To Todd, his boss' voice had always sounded like an old-fashioned washboard. At least it reminded him of the one in the virtual display in the museum on Central Street.

Todd threw his hands up, his frustration about to boil over. "I mean for God's sake, Guy, the man's a loony. He's said a lot of things on my show. You know what psycho's are like. You can't believe half of what they say. You know that."

Guy ground his teeth, a habit that made Todd wince. Todd thought he smelled smoke, even though smoking of any kind hadn't been allowed in office buildings for the past fifty years. "The biggest story in human history, and we coulda had an exclusive."

This pile-on of revelations had taken a toll on Todd's senses — his knees were trembling from too much input, and he sank down onto one of the two steel-framed chairs in front of Guys expansive desk before he collapsed. "Guy. It's not my fault. I mean how was I supposed to know aliens were real? How would anyone know something like that?"

Guy flipped around his flat computer monitor so Todd could see the space ship gaining ground as it raced toward the Earth from the depths of space. The reflective, mirror-like surface of the craft stood out against black of space. An eerie glow surrounded the surface of the ship.

According to the caption scientists from the Jet Propulsion Laboratory in Pasadena said the alien craft was on a trajectory toward the Earth from somewhere outside the solar system. According to telemetry data, just before the alien craft entered the solar system, it reduced velocity from just under the speed of light to a reasonably slower 20,000 KPS, and had been slowing ever since.

Todd shook his head trying to clear this impossible scene from his mind. No, he wasn't dreaming. This was definitely for real; it was happening.

"Get Sikes on the line, and this time I want a straight interview. None of that humiliation crap you're so good at," said Guy, with a thread of deep sarcasm running through his thick voice.

Todd nodded as he watched the screen, transfixed by the events unfolding before his eyes. This was ridiculous. Until now he'd believed in aliens about as much as he believed in Santa Claus. This was going to bring out all the crazies. His show would become a circus. Great for ratings, but he wondered what the longer-term ramifications were going to be.

Guy flipped the screen back toward himself. "You get your ass back into the studio and start planning how you and that pretty little producer of yours are going to handle this. I want an outline of what you plan to do on my desk by the end of day today. Now get the fuck out of my office."

Todd looked at Guy, his mouth agape. He was the star of the station and the network. No one was supposed to speak to him like Guy just did.

Seconds later, Todd stood outside Guy's office after Guy slammed the office door on his ass, too stunned by what just happened to utter actual words. He felt as if he were a shell-shocked war veteran — or at least how imagined a veteran might feel after a battle. He'd never suffered any adverse effects from his time in the military.

The four young reporters, two men and two women, in the khaki overalls that were the latest in fashion among the twenty something's, gazed at him wide-eyed. One by one they rolled their eyes then turned their attention back to their computer screens.

Todd shook off the feeling of helplessness and refocused. It was a technique he'd learned in the Gulf War III to relax after each incursion of his Delta Force team into enemy territory. The United States army taught the rag heads many a bloody lesson in that little dust-up. Too bad the brass hats convinced the president to drop the big one to end it all. He would have loved to have captured the leader of the United Arab League and taught her a lesson or two in manners.

The broad, a very politically incorrect term, but one that best described the machine-gun toting moll, who was as bloodthirsty as they came. At the time he'd wanted one shot at her; but alas, it was never to be. She was dust long before he could get at her.

Making his way back to his producer's cubicle, he found Amy sitting transfixed, her eyes locked on the image on her monitor. Her gray pupils were popped wide, her face pale. She was terrified. The forehead dotted with perspiration, the trembling fingers, the pasty-faced completion as if she were sick and about to vomit. Todd empathized with her. No doubt many people on the planet felt as she did about now. He'd seen too much death in battle to be afraid.

"Unbelievable," she whispered when she noticed him stranding next to her.

"Yeah," he said softly. "Unbelievable. Besides I need to pee — again."

TWO

Mike Sikes sat in his cell staring at the old-fashioned television. Just like they'd promised, the aliens were coming. He wanted to shout for joy at being right and how he was vindicated to all the doubters that called Todd's show and heaped ridicule on him. How he'd shown them.

This was a momentous occasion — the first time anyone in his life had told him the truth. His father and mother were liars of the first order. They'd manipulated him and used his weaknesses against him when he was a child.

His alcoholic father beat him and his mother daily; said repeated beatings would build character in a young man. He never explained about why he beat his mother, and she never protested. Mother was a weak woman.

Mike laughed. Yeah, look how that turned out.

The alien ship was getting closer, and he could hear them inside his head, clearer with each passing hour. Soon, they said, soon.

He smiled to himself. Yup, they'd be here soon and then things would be different.

And he knew who they would see first, but he wasn't telling anyone. No fucking way was he going to talk to anyone except Todd.

The radio host had made fun of him earlier, but that didn't matter. Mike had been honest with him. Sarcasm didn't matter, only truth mattered, and Todd was an honorable man. If anyone understood truth it was Todd Road.

Mike gazed at the old-fashioned telephone the warden had allowed to be installed in his cell. It didn't have a cord attached, like those old museum models. Instead of a series of connecting wires, a miniature transceiver had been built inside the unit so it would operate the same as the modern links. He smirked to himself.

As if he'd kill himself with a cord when he knew his friends were on their way. Until today everyone thought he was crazy, but now they knew better. He glanced at the image on the television again.

Yup, that ship was coming and no power on earth could stop it.

Excitement rose from his belly as he thought about what the pundits would make of him and his revelations now. The rioting would be rampant and the world would fall into chaos. He could hardly wait.

His friends were the good guys. The 'knights in shining armor' types. They were going to get him out of here.

He studied his six-by-nine foot cell, just as he had every day since they'd locked him up. The heavy steel door, with a slit for the guard on patrol to peer in at him at regular intervals, the single bunk with the thin blankets and the lumpy pillow. At least he had the TV and a nightstand full of books. Prisoners had been banned from reading for two decades after too many became jailhouse lawyers and derailed justice. Prisons were not places of justice, they were houses of punishment and societal revenge The warden, who purported to be a Christian, agreed to let him have the books without explanation. This amused Mike no end. The warden was a fool.

He'd mostly been reading science fiction these past few months, since the aliens contacted him. Arthur C. Clarke and Robert J. Sawyer were among his favorites. They wrote about aliens a lot like the ones inside his head. Good, smart, perceptive aliens, not planet-killers like Hollywood portrayed them.

His friends were here to see him. To free him. And Todd Road was going to help them. He just didn't know it yet.

The echo of a voice through the viewing slit in the door interrupted his train of thought.

"Sikes. You got a visitor. Stay where you are."

When the guard activated the unlocking mechanism the steel door creaked and slid open on the steel track, and then into a recessed slot on one side of the doorframe.

Mike stood and held out his hands, palms up, in front of him so the guard could apply the restraining bands to his wrists. The restraints were considered more humane than old-fashioned handcuffs, but they were still uncomfortable.

One guard stepped into the cell, his hand on the butt of his pistol, his dark face was free of any expression as he moved forward and slipped the rubberized restraints over Mike's wrists and uttered the voice-activation command. The restraints immediately tightened around Mike's wrists making full movement of his arms impossible.

After some negotiation with Warden Carter, Mike no longer had to wear the leg restraints while being transported inside the prison walls. The humiliating process of being bound hand and foot then carried from place to place hung from a steel bar as if he were cargo, finally ended with him being allowed to walk like a normal person. A normal person who enjoyed killing people.

The guards were none-too-happy with this arrangement. Even their union had gotten involved by filing a class action grievance with the private owners of the prison facility.

They'd lost and Mike was pleased with the small victory. There weren't many for a man in cellblock triple-X. The other prisoners in the block cheered whenever they saw him go by with the minimal restraints.

A second guard stood outside with his nine millimeter VLE pistol drawn. Mike knew from the look in the silver haired veteran's eyes he wanted Mike to make one wrong move, forcing him to shoot Mike dead. Mike grinned at the second guard when he stepped back to let his partner pass. The large man held Mike by one arm in a grip that made Mike wince.

"Hey!" Mike protested. "Do you have to be so rough?"

The dark skinned guard, in a brown uniform shirt with the Microsoft logo on one shoulder and a Coca Cola log on the opposite arm, smirked at his partner who sneered, but neither said anything in response to their prisoner's protest.

They led him down the hallway, past all the steel doors of his fellow prisoners. None of the slits were open today.

The sunlight made Mike squint. He hadn't seen the sun since his exercise period the previous morning, so it took him several seconds to adjust to the sudden brightness.

Continuing to squint they reached the end of the hallway. The guard told the voice encrypted door to open.

It slid open and they started down the corridor past another row of cells. There were forty-seven such wings in this prison.

At the end of the corridor they turned left and through another steel door. This led into a brightly lit room with round metal tables surrounded by matching gray steel chairs.

At one table, sitting by herself, was his lawyer, Holly Wodson. She was on the high side of thirty, unmarried (as he'd learned through his own interrogation) who enjoyed romance novels and Vodka martinis, with a twist of lime, not lemon as some people preferred. She insisted on lime, said it tasted better.

Today she wore her best navy pantsuit with a plain white shirt hiding her smallish breasts. Very businesslike, he thought.

Her brown hair was pulled into a bun behind her head revealing a recently acquired suntan from her vacation in Aruba. He imagined her sitting in her lounger reading one of her favorite authors, a martini on a table next to her. He thought of her in a tiny bikini. She was certainly attractive, but too old for his tastes. He liked 'em young.

Her thin red lips remained a grim line as he entered the room in the company of the two burly guards. She stood, her black, soft-sided leather briefcase held in front of her by two red-finger nailed hands, clutching it by its handle as if it were a shield. She didn't like him very much. Not that he cared, he was going to die in the injection room anyway. That was how the system took care of people they considered a problem.

"Hello, Holly. You're looking especially lovely today," he said as he approached the table in the middle of the large room. The scent of her jasmine perfume filled his nostrils.

She nodded, and the guard abruptly shoved him into the seat across the table from her with just a little too much force.

"Watch it, bozo," said Mike, wincing and adjusting his shoulder to ease the sharp pain from the guard's strong fingers pressing into the bone.

"Name's not bozo," said the guard, his voice was deep with an edge of menace.

"Oh, is mister big shot gonna get mad and cry?" Mike relished any chance to taunt these meatheads. They were all muscle and no brains.

The guard's eyes narrowed as if deciding whether or not to stomp the smaller man's ass right into the floor as if he were a nail. Not even the presence of the lawyer seemed to bother him. After several seconds, he shrugged and walked away. Mike knew smacking him around wasn't worth the guard losing his job.

Holly frowned. "Do you have to do that?"

"Do what?" he said innocently.

She ignored his question as she placed her briefcase on the table between them and opened it, pulling out a Federal Appeal Registration Form T666A, which she set in front of him. He recognized the form from his reading the words, THE SUPREME COURT OF THE UNITED STATES in bold capital letters, the name and number of the form beneath this bold declaration, and an embossed images of the U.S. flag and a government seal, typical of these types of bureaucratic forms.

The print was small on the rest of the document. His parents refused laser eye surgery for him when he was a child, a common procedure for children under the age of five, he had difficulty reading the words.

As an adult he always told people he couldn't read. The excuse always caused surprise with his audience, but it was better than if they knew the truth. He read the books in his cell with the aid of a magnifying glass the warden had given him. "Sorry, Holly..." he shrugged.

She rolled her eyes. "Oh, shit. I forgot—" Her cheeks flushed and she turned the document around to face her.

"This is the appeal I've filed with the Supreme Court to stay your execution. It may buy you a few months. Probably until Christmas..."

"I won't be in here that long."

"They won't act before then." She pointed to the document. "They can't..."

"That's not what I mean."

His smug expression caused her cheeks to flush with color, this time with anger, her hazel eyes flaring. "You're not gonna start that alien crap again."

She eased back in her chair. It creaked slightly in the silent room. Mike's eyes flitted to the burly black guard with his lips twisted in a smirk. His partner stood with his hands locked in front of him, his bull-like face expressionless.

The guy could be the King's guard at Buckingham palace for God's sake, he thought. He's a fucking robot.

Mike wore a wry grin on his pale face, his restrained hands sat in his lap. His gray prison jumpsuit was neatly pressed with perfect edges running down his thin arms.

To most people, Mike looked more the college professor who taught an ethics class at Brown University, than a cold-blooded killer. He'd heard her describe him as such to reporters curious about whether he looked like a cold-blooded murderer.

Slight build, shaved head, and mousy appearance added to the perception he was harmless. The gray eyes though, they were always they same. Always cold even when his face said he was happy.

He wanted to laugh. From the beginning of his killing spree he knew he was going die, it was just a matter of place and time. He wanted to control his death.

His eyes shifted to focus once again on Holly.

When he started telling her about aliens from space she said she'd never thought of him as insane. He'd been talking about the aliens for the past three months.

And she told him to stop the calls to the dumb-ass, right-wing Nazi radio guy. She advised him that it didn't help his public any. Not that he cared.

Of course, Todd Road, was using him to boost his status. No doubt Mike's calls had shot the ratings through the roof, resulting in increased revenues for the radio station. His calls benefited them both, Mike got out the word of his innocence, while Todd made buckets of money in ad revenues and became even more famous. The arrangement was a joint project, a symbiotic relationship.

But when he'd told Todd about the aliens, Todd rejected him. Why couldn't the stupid bastard see how great a team they made?

"You've been talking to Road again haven't you?"

He nodded.

"You know how I feel about that. Judges listen to those programs too, you know. I'd bet some of the hawks on the big court listen—"

"I hope so…" He grinned.

"It's not funny!" she snapped. The big black guard scowled at her as she moved forward in her chair and leaned on her elbows across the table. She threw him the okay sign as she regained control of her emotions and lowered her voice. "There's no such thing as aliens."

She looked startled when he laughed.

"Haven't you seen or heard the news today?" he said with a grin.

"No, I listened to a book on mini-disc in my car on the way over… why?"

"Go check out CNN then we'll talk some more. We'll need a whole new defense strategy. It'll be a cold day in hell before they get me strapped to the table now."

Her eyes narrowed. "I'll be back tomorrow."

She stuffed the Federal appeal registration form back in her briefcase then left the room.

***

Hamilton Carter, the warden of Alphaville, the flagship prison of the corporation, the most secure of all prisons in the system world wide, greeted Holly Wodson as she left the prisoner meeting room.

The warden appeared to be in his mid fifties, with gray at the temples of his otherwise black hair. He wore a gray suit and sky blue shirt with matching tie. He was clearly trim and fit for a man of his years. Not that Holly cared for the man or his attitude. She thought he was a little too polished to be a prison warden; but then she hadn't met too many prior to this case. None in fact.

She'd been assigned Mike Sikes's appeal as she had the least experience in criminal law at the firm and no one thought he had a shot at winning. Besides, she needed the experience. Everyone, it seemed, wanted this guy to burn. Of course she shared this view, but she had a job to do. Mike had been different today. Something had fired him up — and she didn't like it when he was happy. Holly shuddered inside, as she did every time she left a meeting with her firm's most despicable client. He frightened her. Her guts twisted when she was in his presence.

"Ms. Wodson," Warden Carter said, with a slight nod of his head and a thin-lipped smile.

Frowning she set her brief case on the white tiled floor next to her right leg. "Hamilton."

When Hamilton Carter introduced himself two years ago, he'd told her to call him by his given name. A courtesy she'd not extended to him.

She enjoyed any advantage over him perceived or otherwise. While she wasn't the best at criminal law she considered herself a skilled litigator.

"What the hell is Mike talking about.... something about television...CNN?"

Hamilton nodded, a small smile fixed to his lips. "The alien ship, of course."

"Has everyone lost their mind today?" She pinched her left arm and shook her head in wonderment. "Nope, I'm awake. I don't get it..."

Hamilton shrugged. "It turns out Mike's not delusional. The Hubble V detected an alien craft headed for Earth. It's all over the news."

Holly felt her knees weaken but managed to remain standing. "Oh my..."

Hamilton nodded his expression grim. "Yeah. I know what you mean."

THREE

For the next two months, Todd sat in the studio straining to hear, and comprehend, every word Mike Sikes said. Sikes appeared on his show every day now since the alien ship had been spotted.

When the cigar shaped craft began to slow, the eggheads at the Jet Propulsion Laboratory, said they were preparing to enter orbit around the Earth. They used the term "geosynchronous orbit," but since he'd failed his senior year physics class in high school, Todd didn't know what they were talking about. A person didn't need physics to be a talk show host.

All he knew for certain was they were finally here, Mike Sikes was the only person they'd contacted on Earth, or so he claimed. He said their intentions were honorable. Of course, that was assuming Todd could rely on the word of a convicted serial killer.

But then Todd seemed to remember saying something about 'honorable intentions' to Becky Wallace's father on the night of the prom, after which he took Becky to the back seat of his Chevy.

Honorable intentions. Right. Mike Sikes might be eating up his airtime, but no way would he believe the manipulative son of a bitch.

At least Guy was beginning to smile when he encountered Todd in the hallways or in the can.

Ratings were way up because the only talk show Mike Sikes spoke to was On the Road with Todd Road. The guys and gals at CNN were foaming at the mouth with jealousy. They frequently called into the show to ask Todd — no, he corrected himself, to beg — for a little time to speak with the latest planet-wide star. Todd imagined the big music stars and celebrity divas were jealous as hell at all the attention he and his big star, Mike Sikes, had garnered.

When he broached the idea of speaking with other reporters with Mike, it met with stony silence followed by a curt, No.

He didn't dare pursue the question further, not wanting to annoy his only guest these past two months.

Every day, after his trite morning monologue, long a trademark of his show, and a ritual he was beginning to think should be exorcised from the program altogether, Amy hooked Mike up by live feed from the Alphaville prison.

If he could have gotten away with it, — and if Guy would have let him — Todd would have eliminated the news, sports, weather, and even the commercials.

After several tense weeks, while the alien craft passed Jupiter, then Mars, and then the Earth's moon, the population of the planet was enveloped by a sense of calm resignation, coupled with uncertainty for the future. What did these aliens want?

Todd was more worried about what they wanted with Mike than anything else.

Azelia Marks, a tourist from Sweden, had been Mike's downfall. The cops traced her to Pitt Town when she used the coast-to-coast, high-speed bus service stop and been able locate witnesses who saw the affable pig farmer talking to her just before she disappeared. Azelia's disappearance cinched the Federal Attorney General's case. But her escape put the nail in Mike's coffin.

The information she provided eventually helped the Feds track Mike down. Using a DNA scanner they found traces of human DNA buried on his land. A careful search by forensic investigators finally uncovered the awful truth.

To everyone in the country, including Todd Road, Sikes was a monster of epic proportions.

Now that the aliens were parked in Earth orbit, the world held its collective breath, waiting to see what would happen next. All the while, Mike Sikes assured everyone their intentions were good. No one was going to get their brain eaten or some such sci-fi nonsense.

"They're out of their cryo-tubes," said Mike.

"Please explain," said Todd, his chin resting on one hand.

"They tell me, but understand I'm no scientist…"

"That's okay. Go ahead."

"Evidently, when you travel near the speed of light, our bodies — theirs are as fragile as ours you understand — are subjected to pressures beyond which we would be unable to tolerate. Simply put, we would be crushed to death before we reached maximum velocity.

"The Pel'Tac — that's what they call themselves — have developed a system of slowing their metabolism for long journeys across interstellar space in something they call a cryo-tube. That's not exactly what they called it, but it's the best way to describe what they told me about their technology. They kind of sleep until they arrive at their destination. But as I explained I'm no scientist."

"Fascinating," said Todd. "What else can you tell us about them?"

"Let's see..." There was a long pause. Dead air space on the radio used to cause listeners to tune in other stations. But Mike had been doing this for weeks, and so far, if the stats guys were correct, no one had tuned out.

If the rating numbers were to be believed, the entire country seemed to be hanging on this man's every word.

"They live in a symbiotic society with another race on their planet," Mike said, breaking the silence. "The other beings are called the Val'Tan. They are best described as the worker bees, similar to the societal structure of the honeybee," explained Mike.

"So they look like bees?"

Now that would be a new one. He didn't recall any of those old vids where the spiny, acid-spitting monsters from space. On the edge of his memory Todd seemed to recall some very early black and white movies, as they were called in the twentieth century, where giant bugs roamed the Earth wreaking havoc. But those bugs weren't from space, at least as he recalled it.

Mike laughed at the question. "No, Todd, they don't resemble monsters, bugs, bees or otherwise."

Todd glanced at the upper right corner of his computer display, where the CNN live feed played in a small box. The image of the cigar-shaped alien ship, its surface reflecting the sun, appeared larger than ever before.

The surface of the ship was completely smooth, unblemished by any sign of antenna, hatchway, or door. There were no running lights, as Earthly aircraft displayed. Maybe there were no navigation problems where they came from.

"So, what do they look like?"

Another long pause. Todd held himself back from speaking. The pauses were driving him a little nuts, but what could he do? For now, Mike controlled the agenda. "Actually, I've never asked them," Mike finally responded, his tone sounding hesitant, almost reluctant.

This was probably the biggest question of the day, if not the century.

Everyone, including the military authorities, wanted to know what these alien beings looked like.

The military brass probably wanted to know how to kill them, too. According to CNN reports, armed forces around the globe were on their highest state of alert short of all-out war.

The talking heads at CNN, along with some well-known science-fiction writers, speculated that any weapons we have would be ineffective against beings who could cross such vast distances. But knowing the military mind as well as Todd did, having been one of them years before, he knew they would throw everything they had in the attempt to stop any would be invaders from space.

"Mike, you and I have spent the past two months talking about the friendship these beings wish to establish with our planet. Can you explain once again why they wanted to come here to pay us a visit?"

They'd been over and over this territory, but each time he told the story, Mike seemed to embellish it with more and more colorful details.

"Todd, I would be pleased to discuss this with you. My lawyer is getting severely pissed at me for discussing any aspect of my case on the radio, but frankly, I don't give a rats butt what she thinks."

Todd chuckled.

"The Pel'Tac are here to free me from prison. They say I'm not responsible for the murders I am alleged to have committed."

Todd winced and his guts twisted as he recalled the circumstances surrounding Mike's case. It was all on the public record. Bloody corpses hacked to pieces, with evidence of brutal torture. There was no escaping the facts, Mike committed the crimes he'd been convicted of.

Court TV covered the trial and broadcast all two hundred and twelve days of testimony.

Victim's families pleaded for the press to stop publicizing it, but the media thirsted for cases like this one like so many blood-sucking vampires, which maybe they were.

Todd got involved when he helped to start a campaign, through his show, to raise money for scholarship funds and other good works arranged by the Society for the Victims of Mike Sikes, a coalition of the families determined to make some good come from his heinous acts. All two hundred and forty three victim's families were involved in the society.

Mike Sikes was without a doubt the worst mass murder in U.S. history.

In fact, outside of war criminals or mad dictators, he alone had committed more individual murders than any single person on record, worldwide. Mike was pure psychopath, that much was clear. But he was also the only person the aliens nearing the planet seemed to be willing to speak to directly.

The politicians and military guys tried to apply pressure to Todd and Guy to give them control of the situation but their efforts had utterly failed. Guy, knowing there were monster ratings in this, stuck by Todd and refused to accept any government offers of assistance. In gov-speak assistance being a thin guise for complete and utter control.

Mike said the aliens would land in the large park in the center of the city, where Todd was to meet them. His radio station would have a live remote link set up — no doubt surrounded by cameras and reporters and multiple squadrons of military personnel — so the KZAP audience, and the network, would hear first-hand the first words exchanged between Todd Road and the alien visitors.

Todd hoped they didn't say anything sappy, like when Armstrong landed on the moon, but he and Amy had worked out a carefully worded greeting to deliver when he went to meet the aliens.

He winced. Stupid. Me meeting aliens? I sound like those idiots in one of those cheap sci-fi movies.

Of course, the military would be there. Probably watching with their satellite systems, the troops, tanks and guns deployed around the landing site ready to pounce if the aliens made the slightest aggressive move. Todd hoped they were peaceful, or he might be the first human disintegrated by their death rays. He felt supremely stupid even thinking about such nonsense.

"Mike, you can't be serious," said Todd straining to keep the skepticism out of his voice. "You've been convicted of the murders and you know you committed them. I mean, com'on...." He cringed. Now I just sound whiny.

Todd could hear the amusement in Mike's reply. "As I've said since day one, I was framed, and I'm innocent. Isn't it ironic that it takes aliens from another world to come here and prove me right?"

"Yeah," said Todd, with a glance at Amy, whose face was twisted in an angry scowl on the other side of the glass wall of the studio.

Instinctively he nodded. Though his guest couldn't see the gesture it helped him to mentally move the interview forward in his own head. He then continued. "Let's change the subject shall we?"

He paused for effect and to create in the mind of the audience a mental break from the discussion of Mike's innocence or guilt. Todd knew his listeners would never believe Mike was innocent any more than he did.

Many of his audience had followed the live television coverage throughout the trial, and later called the program to regale him with the facts of Mike's heinous crimes.

Since Mike started calling the show, even before the alien's appearance, Todd had received death threats from listeners threatening him for letting the serial killer on the program. And now?

Guy would never let him drop Mike now.

"Do you expect the aliens to bring us gifts, such as advances in our own science so we to can travel the stars? Or perhaps medical advances that would cure everything from cancer to the common cold?"

"How would I know?" said Mike, with the equivalent of a verbal shrug.

"Well you must know something about them. Something that would be of benefit to all mankind."

"Not really. All I know is they're here to free me, and that's all that matters to me. I'm innocent." He sounded gleeful.

Innocent? Yeah right. "Time to go to commercial, we'll be back." Todd gently tugged the wax-tainted earpiece from his right ear and eased back in his ergonomic chair. Amy had shut off his on-air microphone system so they could talk to each other off air, out of Mike's hearing.

"If he keeps saying he's innocent we're gonna start losing audience share," said Amy sarcastically, her voice tinny in his left ear. "Aliens or no aliens."

Todd sighed. He glanced at the soundboard embedded in his desk, the monitor set above the board in the console displaying the name of the caller waiting to speak next. His gaze moved over the list of names on the screen. Mike would be eager to spread his garbage. From the list of names it appeared far too many people were anxious to ride the killer's coat tails. How Todd hated celebrities.

"Do you think I should talk to him about the innocent bull?" He shifted to look at Amy as he nodded toward the screen.

"If you do…" she reminded him of his responsibility.

Todd nodded. Amy was right.

Turning his attention back to the board his shoulders slumped. If he pissed the guy off, they might lose him altogether. He'd threatened to go to one of Todd's rivals more than once over the past weeks if he didn't get to say his piece as he chose to say it. Todd hated when a pseudo-celebrity took control of his show. Damn it, this was his show not some crazed killer named Mike Sikes. Unfortunately, the story was now bigger than the host. Not a good thing in this business. Being a personality was everything in talk radio.

A sudden surge of adrenaline welled from inside him that he hadn't felt in twenty-five years. I could use a damn cigarette.

He hadn't thought about cigarettes since the health care riots of 2029 wiped out the tobacco manufacturers, mobs burning all existing tobacco products, plants, and seeds worldwide. Since then, anyone caught with tobacco plant seeds was automatically sentenced to life in prison with no possibility of parole. Not willing to risk serving time in one of those Turkish hell-holes, none of the normally chameleon-like criminal organizations had even tried to black-market the stuff. Nope, cigarettes were a dead issue.

The drug companies made a fortune with their replacement therapies; so at least someone was happy, fat, and rich. Truth, justice, and the American way went on.

Amy tapped on the glass between them interrupting his thoughts. He hadn't heard her frantic calls over his other earpiece.

"What?" he said annoyed at having been brought back from his daydream. He stole a glance at the monitor and saw the alien craft with the moon behind it clearly outlined against the slate gray surface of that dead world.

"We're on in ten," he heard Amy say in his earpiece.

He fumbled with the other earpiece and stuffed it in his ear just as the ten seconds, showing on his monitor at the bottom of the screen in neon red letters, expired. He pushed the button to activate the on air microphone.

“Okay, we’re back live with Mike Sikes. Mike, the alien ship carrying your friends the Pel’Tac is very near the Earth now. Perhaps you can tell us more about this symbiotic race the Val’Tans. What are they like and how do the Pel’Tac need them? As I understand symbiotic relationships, each needs the other to survive.”

“I’m not entirely clear on that myself, Todd, but I’ll give an explanation a try, at least as I understand it.”

Mike went on the better part of ten minutes explaining the Pel’Tac and Val’Tan’s symbiosis. It seemed the Val’Tans excreted a chemical substance from their bodies, which was highly toxic when released into the air, and would kill them in excessive amounts. Fortunately, that same substance was similar to a very necessary chemical lacking in the brain tissues of the Pel’Tac.

After a refining process, which the Pel’Tac said was too complicated to explain to humans, they ingest the resulting chemical into their bodies, which then travels to certain centers of their brains and keeps them sane.

Without the chemical a severe form of what they described as schizophrenia would overwhelm them. Madness and chaos would end their civilization, and death would be the end result. If they were unable to obtain the secretions of the Val’Tans, the Pel’Tac estimated their entire race would become extinct in less than fifty of their years.

Likewise, if the Pel’Tac were unable to use the substance for any useful purpose it would rise to toxic levels in their atmosphere, killing off the Val’Tans in an even shorter period of time. The two races need each other to survive.

Mike summed up his explanation. “Maybe if that had been the case on Earth the world would be a far better place than it is.”

“That’s very interesting, Mike. I wonder what any of this has to do with you.”

“It’s really rather simple, Todd.” Mike spoke Todd’s name as if he were speaking to a small child. Todd’s gut tightened in anger, but he quickly suppressed it. “The Pel’Tac know an injustice when they see one. They want me to have that justice.”

Todd knew that explanation didn’t make any sense, but he hesitated to argue with his number one guest. It occurred to him Mike might be hiding something. But what? Or he just might be nuts. “There had to be more to it than that. I mean why travel all that way just to seek justice for one man?”

“Todd, Todd, Todd…” Now he was patronizing him. Todd ears grew warm. “These are aliens, for God’s sake. They have a different moral code than we have. That’s why we call them aliens.”

A loud rap on the glass made Todd glance toward the producer’s booth. Amy was standing, staring at him with two people in dark clothing standing behind her. A man and a woman, their faces hard and their cold eyes fixed on him.

The dark-skinned man wore a dark suit and blue shirt, no tie, his hands clasped in front of his trim waist. The red-haired woman beside him wore a black leather jacket over a snow white shirt, open at the neck. Her smooth, fair skin was brushed lightly with rouge on her high cheekbones. Her pale green eyes stared at him and her full red lips were pursed in a way that suggested she was not happy.

Todd nodded at Amy who threw her hands up.

“Mike, we’re going to have to break away now, and join CNN live as the aliens are about to arrive in Earth orbit.

"As we agreed, I'll meet with them in two days. Can we talk some more afterwards?"

"Yeah. Of course, buddy."

Todd cringed inside. Crap. He called me buddy. Todd went to the door between the two rooms, opened it, and stepped into the producer's booth. Amy had switched over to the CNN feed coming from the hidden speakers above their heads. The excited voice of the reporter — those guys were usually so calm — explained the alien vessel was about to pass near the Hubble V in orbit high above the Earth.

Amy turned the sound down so it was only a low background noise in the suddenly crowded room.

The man reached into his back right pants pocket and extracted a black leather wallet, flipping it open to reveal a large, gold-colored badge and identification card. In large block letters of blue script, the card identified him as FBI. "I'm Agent Williams, this is Agent Cody," said the man, nodding at his partner whose hard features morphed briefly to provide a brief humorless smile.

"We'd like to speak with you in private, Mr. Road."

Todd had anticipated the FBI would get interested since Mike started talking his crazy shit though it puzzled him why they took so long. I guess they don't believe in aliens either.

All the time he'd wondered what to say to the feds when they showed up with their questions. Problem was, he didn't really know anything. How would he explain any of this?

"Sure, follow me," he said. He nodded at Amy who sat down and sighed, obviously relieved the government didn't want anything to do with her.

"We'll be back to interview you as well, Ms. Rickland," said Agent Cody, before they left the booth and headed down the hallway to Todd's office. He demanded and received his own office in the last contract negotiations. The station owner had given in easily. Did that concession ever piss off Guy. On air talent never got their own office.

Right now it was the middle of the day, so from the large picture window Todd could see the river teeming with boats, tugs, and freighters of all sizes.

The two bridges were filled with cars, trucks and buses, carrying people about as they went about their daily lives oblivious to the events unfolding above their planet — or those in the lavish office of Todd Road.

The odor of the tuna fish sandwich he'd had delivered for lunch still filled the air as each of the FBI agents took a seat in the leather office chairs in front of his dark-stained oak desk.

Todd's back was to the window as he sat in his leather executive chair. He clasped his trembling hands in his lap. They were moist with perspiration.

"Want anything, coffee? Tea? Soft drink?" he offered with a slight grin on his flushed face. Was it hot in here or was it just him?

Williams waved away the offer with one hand and shook his head. "We're fine." His partner said nothing, keeping her green eyes focused on him, causing his stomach to churn. "So, what can I do for you?" he said when Williams and Cody were silent for several seconds.

"We understand you intend to meet the aliens in the park the day after tomorrow. Is this correct?" said Cody. She leaned forward in her chair, resting her weight on one arm. Until now, Todd thought the guy was in charge. Obviously he'd been wrong. What we do when we assume.

"Yes. Mike said.... "

Cody scowled. "Don't believe anything that piece of shit says.... "

"Angela," said Williams with caution in his deep voice.

Cody sat back in her chair, her demeanor reverting to the calm persona of a few seconds before. "Mr. Road. Mike Sikes is a cold-blooded killer, and I would know," said the red-headed agent.

"And why is that?" said Todd, now genuinely curious about this woman.

"I'm the one who caught the son of a bitch."

FOUR

THE BLONDE CNN REPORTER's blue eyes stared unblinking into the camera as she read the teleprompter.

"The spacecraft, now known by everyone in Todd Road's listening audience as the Pel'Tak ship, arrived in Earth orbit at 0916 Greenwich Mean Time.

"All attempts by the military and civilian authorities at communication have been met with stony silence. The craft did deposit a series of silver, ball-shaped objects in orbit around the Earth. This has been confirmed by satellite reconnaissance.

"Each is the size of a baseball, and each parked itself at a stationary position for what purpose no one knew. Apparently not even Mike Sikes knew what the Pel'Tak are doing with these objects.

"For the past two days, the world has held its collective breath, until finally, just a few minutes ago, a smaller craft separated from what the pundits called 'the mother ship' and headed for the park near the KZAP studio, and Todd Road, are located.

"Now maybe world will get some answers. Stay tuned to CNN for breaking news on the day we knew we are not alone.

"This is Beth Aimes reporting live from Washington."

***

Todd stepped from the men's room, where he'd quickly used the toilet and washed his hands — and checked to ensure the FBI listening device was properly secured to his suit jacket.

Today he wore a gray suit, his personal favorite, with a dark red shirt done up at the collar. He decided not to wear the tie that went with the ensemble. Too old-fashioned.

He'd even had a barber re-shave his head and apply a thin layer of wax to make him appear, quite literally, polished and professional.

He held his breath and slowly exhaled, then headed for the elevators at the end of the hallway. A gaggle of reporters and his fellow station personnel were gathered in the hallway watching him go by.

Some smiled thinly while others stared at him like he was the bravest man on the planet. This can't be happening.

He twisted his shoulders beneath his suit jacket to let the finely tailored material fall naturally into place. He rubbed his moist hands down the sides of his trousers as he arrived at the bank of three elevators. They would carry him to the lobby, where he'd board the limousine for the short ride to the meeting.

Guy stood nearby, a big grin fixed to his craggy features. He stuck out one hand, and grasped Todd's upper arm firmly in the other as he shook his hand vigorously. "This is my man," he said his rough voice strangling the words.

Todd winced at a sharp twinge in his shoulder as Guy let go of his hand and then slapped him on the back with the flat of his meaty hand. Guy was no youngster, but he worked out every day, and it showed. The two men entered the elevator car together.

The doors closed and Guy's smile disappeared. "Road, you fuck this up and you'll never work in radio, or anywhere else inside the continental United States. You understand me?"

Todd's hands began to sweat and his belly knotted with fear. He nodded at his boss and again wiped his moist hands on his trouser legs. This week's stellar ratings were little protection, he knew. Guy would fire him flat out if he screwed up. Radio was fast becoming a younger man's game. Who would hire a fifty-five year old radio host who'd been fired after he appeared to befriend a serial killer? No one.

They arrived in the lobby and Guy's wide smile reappeared as soon as the door slid aside, revealing a crowd of humanity held back by a wall of policemen and women dressed in their finest uniforms, with peaked hats, polished brass buttons that ran in a row down the center of their navy-blue jackets, and snow-white gloves.

The two FBI agents, Angela Cody and Lenard Williams, stood to one side watching the circus unfold. Cody nodded at Todd as he passed, her expression serious.

Bursts of light came from the nest of news videographers as virtual cameras followed them to the street.

The odor of burning fossil fuel — a rare thing these days, given the extreme expense of gasoline — hung over the front of the building, where a large, white limousine sat parked by the curb. A uniformed driver in a dark suit and white gloves sat behind the steering wheel, his eyes focused forward, waiting for them. The man didn't even glance up as Guy opened the door and hustled Todd into the back seat.

There was a ring of identical benches surrounding a knee level table in the middle of rear passenger compartment, complete with drink holders inlaid into the black plastic surface.

Todd slid across the plush, crushed, red velvet seats to the far side of the rear bench, Guy dropped in heavily beside him and slammed the car door after him.

Sitting across from him, Todd was shocked to see a woman wearing a tan business suit. She was attractive and slim, with chestnut-brown hair that draped over her shoulders, and intense hazel eyes that stared at him as if he were a maggot. Her thin red lips were pursed and her face was pinched.

She didn't like him, and she didn't even know him. Of course, some people who knew him didn't like him much either. Sometimes it bothered him, but with all that had happened since this nightmare began, he was really beyond caring what people thought of him.

She held out one peach nail-polished hand to offer to shake his. "You must be Mr. Road," she said, in a husky voice.

"Huh…yes. You are?" He raised one eyebrow.

She glanced up and down at him as if he were an ugly dress in the window of some homely person's clothing store. "I'm Mr. Sikes's attorney —"

"Holly Wodson," interrupted Todd.

She raised one eyebrow, looking mildly surprised he even knew her name, and turned to glance out the window at the pedestrians they were passing on the sidewalk. There was no traffic ahead or behind them. A gauntlet of police air cars and sky cycles had cleared the road and snarled traffic for miles in every direction from the center of the city.

The downtown core would be a congested mess. That didn't matter to the politicians who ran the city of course. They played up big in the media that theirs was the first place visited by aliens from outer space.

Todd knew they'd erect statues and monuments to mark the event. Maybe they'd even have one of him soon.

I'm a talk show host, damn it. My ratings weren't very good until all this happened. All he wanted was his little radio show and a small "c" celebrity status, nothing more. Todd was a Midwest boy with a dream of working in radio, but now he was the spokesperson for the entire planet. The responsibility threatened to overwhelm him.

"Mike told me all about you, Ms. Wodson."

"Yes, I'm sure he did," she said dryly.

Guy visibly fumed, crossing his arms across his chest. There was an uncomfortable silence the rest of the way to the park.

The limo pulled up in front of an area where a colorful green and red tent had been erected to act as the staging area for the dignitaries and press corps who were present to greet the visitors from space.

The mayor, the vice-president, and assorted military officers, in their best dress uniforms, stood milling about, each with a drink of juice. (No one would risk consuming alcohol today and chance dulling their senses or making fools of themselves) They munched on taxpayer funded hors d'oeuvres laid out by the finest restaurants in the state. Todd smirked. Wherever you find free food, a politician was sure to follow.

They stepped out of the limo into the morning air, and were enveloped by the scent of flowers in their last bloom of the summer. The yellow, red, and tangerine roses, bright orange begonias, and golden black-eyed Susan's that lined the flowerbeds surrounding the meadow where the alien craft would land were like a feast for the eyes.

The dignitaries and military men broke from their private sidebars when they saw Todd and Guy coming toward them followed by Holly Wodson.

A man in a black-and-gold fleece vest, a white apron tied around his waist, carrying a tray of various juices, intercepted them when they were almost at the tent.

His ruddy complexion broke into a smile, the thin dark moustache over his upper lip twisting at the corners and his gray eyes sparkling. "Mr. Road. Is there anything I can get you, sir? Anything at all."

"Huh…no thanks. I'm gonna wait in the tent."

"Of course, Mr. Road, I understand, sir. Please follow me."

The man turned away, his back now to them. He held the tray still upright, not spilling a drop and led them inside the tent.

It reminded Todd of a circus tent with the drape of the sides falling away as if supported from the middle by a post, though there was none he could see.

Once inside he saw there were three, unoccupied, steel-framed gray chairs, each with a pale blue cushion on the seat. Todd glanced at his Rolex as he sat down. Thirty-two minutes before they arrived.

The dignitaries around him avoided his gaze and went back to their private conversations. He wasn't popular with the establishment right now. Talk show hosts acquainted with serial killers were a bad mix in many of the public's minds.

They were none-too-pleased that it was Todd Road that had been picked by aliens to be the Earth's representative.

"Everything'll be fine," whispered Guy who sat beside him with his legs crossed and his arms at his sides. He grinned at Todd.

Todd studied the various men and women milling about. Even the civilians looked like brass. Todd squirmed in his seat and a trickle of perspiration ran down his back. He was way over his head in dignitary and he didn't like it. How had he gotten himself into this situation?

Finally the time arrived to walk to the side of the meadow where the alien ship was supposed to land. NORAD reported that the alien craft was on the outskirts of the city and would be here within five minutes.

Todd heard the sound of jet engines and thought at first that it must be from the alien ship. But no, they actually sounded more like F33 military jets, like the ones he'd seen at air shows when he was a kid. Only these were the pilotless models, far more powerful and deadly than any earlier version.

Sure enough two sleek gray fighter jets screamed overhead followed by the alien ship. It was silver like its mother ship, shaped much the same, though a smaller version of the silver cigar. It didn't make a sound and there was no visible exhaust. Somehow he'd expected a fiery landing similar to the ones in some Hollywood movies. Instead this ship had no visible signs of a propulsion system. The big brains were no doubt going to study this craft for decades to determine how it worked.

As the ship approached the ground, strut-like extensions appeared to melt from the craft to form a tri-pod landing arrangement. The ship set down slowly, noiselessly, in the middle of the meadow, the struts extended from the main body sighing as the craft settled and stopped moving.

Todd spotted a reflective glint from the edge of the trees that lined the meadow. No doubt trained snipers were sitting out there, watching and waiting, ready to shoot to kill. He didn't know if the military intended hurting, or planned to protect, the aliens. There had been threats to kill the aliens when they landed, even to bomb the park by fringe nut jobs.

Todd ran the palm of one hand over his damp brow wiping away the beads of accumulated sweat, then moved closer to the ship.

Guy stayed by the tent, as did Holly Wodson; Guy's eyes wide and his mouth hanging open. Knowing him like Todd did, Guy had probably thought this was all an elaborate hoax until the evidence was sitting not fifty yards away.

Todd thought he should say something profound. Instead he jumped back as a ramp of sorts extended from the craft and a doorway appeared in the side of the ship. The way this thing was able to change its shape made him wonder if it was made of liquid instead of metal. Or liquid metal? His eyes were wide with amazement. This was way too surreal.

He moved forward slowly on trembling legs, wiping his sweaty palms on his pant legs. His knees shook and his stomach churned. The sour taste of bile rose at the back of his throat. He had never been so scared in all his life.

"Weird day, isn't it?"

"You can say that again," he muttered under his breath.

"What?" shouted one of the reporters who held a directional microphone up aimed directly at him.

He stopped. Whoever had spoken hadn't said it out loud. The voice was inside his head. It had the oddest accent — an odd mixture of Irish and Japanese, as if that made any sense.

"Who said that?" he said taking a step toward the recently constructed silver ramp.

"I did," said the reporter.

"Not you—you asshole," said Todd angrily.

"Watch the language," said the voice inside his head. "Not good for your blood pressure."

The voice sounded gentle. Todd felt a sense of relief wash over him. This was going to work out. "Come inside. Trust us."

It was clear to him they wanted him to come inside their ship.

He gingerly put one Florshiem on the ramp to test it for solidity. It was firm and dry. He felt a slight give to the ramp's surface, like when you stepped on sand at the beach, but it would certainly be capable of holding the weight of his pudgy body.

He grinned then started up the ramp. Maybe this wasn't going to be so big bad and scary after all.

He waved for the gathered reporters and gave Guy a thumb's-up sign. Guy was standing under the tent, gazing after him with a look of stunned amazement on his face. He gave an involuntary thumb's-up.

Todd smiled to himself then strode into the interior of the alien craft and out of sight of the watching world.

The ramp slid inside the ship, and with it the doorway Todd disappeared into, replaced by the unblemished silver surface of the Pel'Tak vessel. It was as if both the doorway and the ramp had never existed.

Todd Road had officially gone where no talk show host had gone before.

FIVE

On the six-inch video screen the Alphaville warden had allowed him for this event, Mike saw Todd Road disappear inside the alien craft. He shook his head in amazement.

Todd really did it. He went aboard the Pel'Tak ship.

Mike hadn't thought the smarmy talk show host's corpulent body contained sufficient guts to do something like that, but there it was, for all the world to see. Some people just surprised you when they did something outside their true nature. It wouldn't be long before Todd discovered his lies about the Pel'Tak. He smirked.

So what if Road did? There was very little the radio host could do about it now.

It was true that the Pel'Tak lived in a symbiotic relationship with the Vel'Tan, and that they survived the trip to Earth inside some kind of device they called a stasis field (the cryo-tube thing was his own invention), but beyond that he knew very little about them.

His fantastical descriptions of their society was just good radio, and if Todd was gullible enough to believe him, and to pass off his version of truth to his listeners without question, then who was Mike Sikes to argue?

Besides it had been fun to keep the guy on the hook like some overweight trout. About the only thing he had in common with Todd Road was they were both hairless. His by the design of nature, Todd's by choice.

Now Todd was going to meet the aliens first hand and he'd soon be out of this god-forsaken dump and free to live his life as he chose, and not as the cattle out there decided. His eyes narrowed as he watched the silver ramp disappear inside the ship. He smiled thinly.

His plan was unfolding exactly as he envisioned it would. How he loved the game of manipulation, he'd even conned some aliens. Who in history had ever done that?

***

Todd stood inside the smooth-walled room. It glowed with a soft white light, as if the walls themselves were backlit. He studied the walls and ceiling. The room he stood in was almost translucent, but seemed solid enough underfoot. He was alone.

"Hello…" his voice echoed off the walls reflecting back at him. There was no response so he tried again. "Hello?"

He nearly jumped out of his black leather loafers as the wall in front of him seemed to change before his eyes and became a doorway. A being (for lack of a better description), that appeared much too human, stepped into the room. He wore a gray suit that looked like it came from Neiman Marcus and a white shirt with a sky-blue tie. On the alien's feet — he had only two, and two arms — were shoes that looked identical to Todd's own Florshiems.

"Nice tailor..." Todd muttered. He stopped in mid-thought as he looked into the being's eyes. They were deep red, with no white to mark the edges. It made the 'man' appear like a freakish 'little Orphan Annie.'

Hello. The man's — at least he looked like a man — face didn't betray any expression, his lips didn't move when he spoke yet Todd could hear him clearly.

"Humm...welcome to our planet," said Todd, feeling a little queasy in the pit of his stomach. Were they moving? He thought for a second the ship was moving under his feet. Or was the sensation in his head?

"Are we going somewhere?"

The man-being bowed at the waist, his arms at his sides. Thank you and yes.

They were leaving the park. He didn't recall this being part of the deal, to be kidnapped by the aliens. Then again what was the deal? Mike hadn't said more than the aliens would meet him in the park. He erupted in a sudden burst of anger mixed with numbing fear. They were going to suck out his brains or something. Damn it, he was an American. They couldn't do that, he had rights.

No, Mr. Road, we're not going to suck out your brain. It was the voice inside his head again. He knew somehow this wasn't the voice of the man-being in front of him There was an edge of amusement in the voice this time. Certainly this voice in his head was more expressive than the statue-like man-being gazing at him with the creepy, unblinking red eyes.

Todd suppressed his anger and his heart rate decreased. "What are you guys?" He pointed at the man-being in the gray suit with the red eyes.

"That guy,' as you call him, Mr. Road, is a Vel'Tan, didn't Mr. Sikes explain?

Todd nodded. "Yeah, sorta..."

Oh my, said the voice. There was a momentary pause. I think you've been misinformed.

"What do you mean?"

Feeling braver, now that he was communicating with someone, albeit an unseen someone, Todd moved around the statue-like, red-eyed, man-being. He reached out with one finger and pressed against the stationary figure's left arm. There was a mild electric current in the tip of his finger where it made contact with the man-being's arm. It was an odd sensation.

The red-eyed man-being didn't blink, nor did his eyes follow Todd as he moved slowly around him. His various appendages and limbs appeared to be in the right places but he definitely wasn't human. His skin was unnaturally pink, perhaps as it should be, but he didn't seem to be breathing. He was startled when the man suddenly took in a deep breath and his chest heaved then he exhaled the air as if he were clearing his lungs. He didn't inhale another breath, standing unmoving as before.

"This isn't a real man, is it?" said Todd.

No.

"What is it?"

It's a little hard...we thought Mr. Sikes would've explained all this to you by now, the voice sounded distressed.

"Yeah. You said that already. Now what gives?" Todd frowned, resting balled fists on his ample hips. Superior race my ass. These people were really beginning to piss him off.

We understand your confusion, Mr. Road. As you can appreciate we share your concerns.

The guy must be a bureaucrat, because it sounded like bullshit to him. He considered asking to leave, and made a move toward the wall where the doorway to the outside used to be.

Sorry, Mr. Road, but you can't leave at the moment. You see —

Todd finally lost his cool. "Now you listen to me. No little green men from space are going to hold a citizen of the United States of America hostage. Under the rules of the Geneva Convention —" he stopped. The Geneva Convention probably didn't apply to this situation, but what the hell it was worth a shot. "Under the rules of the Geneva Convention we have the right to life, liberty and the pursuit of happiness. We —"

No. No, please, Mr. Road, said the voice in an attempt to calm him down, but Todd had run out of things to say anyway. He didn't know the actual wording of the Geneva Convention. His breath came heavy from between his thin pale lips. His face was flushed as the air temperature had increased considerably from outside. He undid the top button of his shirt. The man-being still hadn't moved.

All will be explained when we meet, assured the voice.

"And when will that be?" said Todd indignantly.

In about ten of your minutes when the vessel you are aboard will dock with my star ship. The 'red eyed, man-being', as you call him, will take you to what is best described, in terms you will understand, as my office.

Todd had to be the first talk show host in space. I'm gonna be rich on the movie, book, and television rights, he realized. Beads of perspiration sprang out of his forehead quickly forming rivulets than ran down the sides of his face. That was of course if he didn't have a heart attack from the stress he felt right now.

Not yet, Mr. Road.

Todd cringed. God, he thought, I've only known these guys for a few minutes and I detest having my mind invaded already.

***

True to their word the smaller vessel reached the mother ship within ten minutes and the red-eyed man-being led him through a maze of silver corridors to a room the size of a football stadium. It was empty, except for a raised dais in the center of the room. On the dais, which appeared to float above the floor, was a ball, made of glass, with some sort of sparkling creature inside. The creature blinked like Christmas lights as it floated suspended above a console.

Todd was no scientific brain, but even he could tell these people's technology was far ahead of anything on Earth.

Welcome, Mr. Road, said the voice.

Todd covered his ears and grimaced at the pain as the voice in his head became intolerably loud.

Sorry, Mr. Road. Is that better?

He nodded and lowered his hands from his ears as the modulation level lessened. They'd turned down the volume.

"Yeah," he said, his voice echoing off the walls. The surrounding auditorium (he decided that's what the large structure surrounding the dais reminded him of most) was snow-white and glowed with an inner light.

Maybe this was what heaven looked like. All antiseptic, and clean. At least these were neat aliens. No dripping goo or other messy substances. The place didn't even have an odor to it, not even pine cleaner, though it appeared as pristine as a hospital. In fact there wasn't a smell of any kind. I wonder how they keep the place so sanitary.

Mr. Road, my name is...

But Todd was lost in his own world, staring at the ball of filaments floating at eye level. The voice in his head must be coming from the object, as the thin, spider-web like filaments seemed to fluctuate and flow in rhythm to the fluctuation as if mimicking speech.

Curious.

The intermittent patterns fascinated him.

Mr. Road, are you paying attention?

The words made him start, as if he were in a dream. "Huh… sorry. It's just I've never seen a ball of spider webs talk before. Please excuse me. What were you saying?"

He thought for a second the voice chuckled then it continued. As I was saying my name is…

The name it gave was unpronounceable but it sounded as if it began with the letter p and ended with an e. The closest he could come to giving it a name that he would be able to say was Pie. He decided to call the alien Pie.

He heard a soft sigh inside his head. If you must. The alien sounded resigned but mildly annoyed.

He'd never considered that aliens would be annoyed at something so trivial until he recalled his experience in high school when the other kids in his grade eight class made fun of his name by dubbing him road kill.

"Huh…sorry…Pie," he said sheepishly.

Mr. Road, you are in the control center of our vessel. This red eyed man-being as you call him is a Vel'Tan. He is what you would call a mechanical engineer. He keeps our vessel operating at prime efficiency.

His name is… Another unpronounceable name. A real tongue twister. Todd decided to call him Pal.

He will accompany you when you meet Mr. Sikes.

"Hold on," said Todd, the anger in his voice reflecting off the snow-white walls of the room. "Meet Sikes? I don't think so… I talk to the guy on my talk show…I'm not going into any dirty prison…." His stomach knotted and his mouth dried.

"Mr. Road, you are the one person on this planet who talks directly with Mr. Sikes. We believe he is innocent of the crimes with which he's been charged. We need your help to prove this."

Todd was able to stop himself before he laughed out loud. Outrageous. The last thing Mike was is innocent. Mike must have been telling these aliens they were friends or some-such nonsense. Hard to believe a race that could travel between the stars couldn't comprehend a man like Mike Sikes.

The feds, too, had said they needed Todd to help them. He realized the FBI actually needed him because he was the point of contact to these aliens. Agent Wodson assured him that the United States government would make his cooperation worthwhile.

He had an odd sense of disbelief he was even considering these offers, but the aliens seemed to be the larger of the two threats right now so he decided he better sign-on and help the feds when — and if — he could. It would be a balancing act he'd somehow manage between the feds and the aliens.

After he'd gained the cooperation of the aliens, and brought them under control of the government, the Feds had promised that the Federal Communications Commission ruling committee would rule in his favor on a number of pending complaints against him concerning the at-times dicey language and content on his show.

He should have told the FBI that as a patriot all they had to do was ask and he would have been happy to cooperate in anyway possible. Silencing the FCC was a bonus so he let them make the offer anyway.

He smiled nicely at the two agents when he agreed to help them.

I'm certainly in demand, he mused.

But the FBI had one stipulation: Wodson told him to tell the aliens that Sikes would not be allowed out of prison. According to what Mike had told investigators who interviewed him after the appearance of the alien craft, they wanted him released so they could conduct their own investigation and prove his innocence.

The FBI also wanted to know why the aliens believed Sikes was innocent when they had irrefutable proof he'd committee the murders. DNA scans did not lie. Todd agreed.

Mike must have told them that he believed himself innocent and that he'd been framed by a massive government conspiracy. It was a shtick...

What's a shtick? asked Pie.

"Huh...it's.... it means I agree in my native language," he said. They must read minds. How much do they know about me?

Pie's voice sounded curious. I thought we knew all Earth languages....

"It's Brooklynese," explained Todd. He couldn't tell them that he'd manufactured his belief in Mike's innocence for ratings. How do you explain ratings to aliens who'd probably never heard of radio?

Todd, like most of America, had been horrified at the savagery of the killings; dismemberment at the time of death, blood rituals, and mutilation of the victim's sex organs.

Who would have thought a pig farmer from the Midwest would be slaughtering transient women from across America and Canada? Even some tourists.

Now these strangers from another planet come along to declare his innocence? Todd chuckled under his breath.

It was a load of bull that would increase his ratings a hundred fold or more.

Oh. Regional dialect?

"Very." Todd cringed inside. It was becoming evident to him these beings may think they know everything about Earth. They'd probably been watching too much vid. The five thousand channel universe and still nothing on. But they didn't know the subtlety of living among humans. It dawned on him that this was a tidbit of knowledge about them that might work to his advantage.

"When does your man, Pal want to meet with Sikes?"

The ball glowed brightly. He wondered if this indicated they were happy.

Why not now? said Pie, his tone excited.

Todd nodded. "When can we be back on Earth?"

Pie used the unpronounceable name of his air car mechanic again. Come to think of it Todd's Greek mechanic's name was virtually unpronounceable, too. Todd smiled to himself.

"Pie, could we call him Pal, please? It makes it easier for me to pronounce."

If you think that would help. There was a pause.

Just like a real conversation except it's more like talking to yourself. Todd thought he was finally losing his grip on reality. The ordered, simple world he'd built for himself, where common sense rules applied, had finally been turned on its head.

He'll follow your instructions to the letter from now on. I've downloaded a personality matrix into him, which you should find pleasant. I modeled him after one of your movie heroes. From our observations you seem to revere these types.

For a second Todd almost thought Pie was mocking him. He dismissed the thought. Aliens don't mock.

Todd frowned. He hoped bringing the alien back with him wasn't going to be a problem — for him. Somehow he thought he saw trouble with a capital T in the fog ahead.

"Okay, Pal. Lead the way."

If the alien, who stared unblinking at him, had a sense of humor, which from his blank expression he didn't, he would have thought Todd sounded as ridiculous as he felt.

Todd followed close behind Pal, his face warm. No doubt it was offering a contrast to the whiter walls surrounding them.

Pal was now dressed in a one-piece grey coverall that ended at his pale pink neck, which stuck out to hold his hairless, egg-shaped head. On his feet he wore what appeared to be black, calf-high boots, and they looked soft to the touch.

As they passed through the arch it seemed to melt, as if the walls were bleeding ahead of them to spill them into the maze of corridors beyond.

Todd knew he'd better stay close to Pal. He was certain he'd lose his way if he didn't have a guide. He hoped they were headed toward the smaller ship and then back to Terra Firma. He was no space man, for God's sake.

He could hardly believe he was in the presence of aliens on their space ship. If he didn't know better, he would think he was dreaming. He had to hold himself back from pinching himself.

The networks had to be salivating with jealousy. He smiled as he followed the human-like alien down the corridor, their footsteps echoing off the plain, smooth-as-glass walls. The walls looked like glass but they didn't reflect any light. It occurred to him he hadn't seen a light source of any kind. Of course, what did he know about aliens?

This might be fun until it dawned on him who he was about to meet, face-to-face, someone as alien to Earth as any of these creatures. Mike Sikes.

SIX

PAL SAT ON A SEAT THAT EXTENDED from the floor as if it were part of the ship, not something separate. Evidently the walls around them could change shape at will in order to accommodate the wishes of the occupant. These aliens were masters in their environment.

Todd hoped they wouldn't be able to take control of his world as easily as it appeared they could theirs.

He watched as Pal waved his hands over a control surface extending from the side of the chair. The high-backed chair Pal had created for him to sit on moved beneath him. He looked around the smooth surface of the chair and discovered there was no seat belt. Guess they don't have accidents.

There was no view screen so he had no idea where they were or how long it would take to reach the prison complex.

The Alphaville prison was a series of buildings constructed in a hexagon around a central, park-like hub. The prison housed the worst terrorists, murderers, rapists, and war criminals from the four corners of the planet, so the security systems were state of the art. And while the corporation employed some human guards, the security features of the prison were mostly automated.

A DNA encoded chip carrying a mini-bomb had been inserted in each prisoner's brain.

The chip could be activated at any time, so if the prisoner escaped they could be tracked, If they were able to evade capture after being free more than twenty four hours, they were deemed lost and the chip would be activated. Their central nervous system would overload, and they would die immediately, wherever they were on the planet. Escape meant instant death

Only one inmate had ever escaped since the prison was constructed. Twenty four hours after he managed to get away, the chip was activated and his body liquefied. It certainly made the clean-up simple.

Wash away your troubles, were the words Todd used to describe the event for his listeners.

He smirked to himself as he recalled the end of Lenny Leibowitz, child killer. Good riddance to bad seed. Lenny didn't suffer now did he? Not like his child victims.

No one had successfully escaped since bad 'ol Lenny. In fact none had even tried. Instant death without benefit of appeal was a pretty good deterrent.

He glanced at Pal. The being that, until now, had pretty much the appearance of a robot seemed more animated. He broke into a hum. He was humming an oddly familiar tune. A favorite of Todd's from the late twentieth century.

"You know that song?" said Todd. The talking-via-brain crap was getting on his nerves. He hated aliens rattling around in his head. He wondered though if they had limits since Pal didn't seem to know everything he was thinking, at least the alien didn't comment on everything he thought.

Pal turned and focused his red eyes on Todd. The alien blinked, surprising him. His stony features broke into a wide smile but the eyes remained absent of any sign of life.

"What the fuck..." whispered Todd. The grinning alien looked like a demon about to consume his soul. "Cut that out," he said angrily. "You're creeping me out."

The alien appeared puzzled for a moment then the false smile disappeared. The alien's brow was furrowed.

"I thought humans smiled," he said out loud.

Todd had never been so relieved as when Pal starting speaking out loud. To him it seemed unconstitutional to invade a mind without permission.

"It's not that...it's just that I didn't expect you all of a sudden becoming so animated is all."

The alien looked confused. Obviously he didn't know anything about human communication.

Well, if he was gonna survive his little visit to our backwater planet then I'm gonna have to give him a crash course in 'human'. Todd sighed and stood up from the chair.

"That would be appreciated," said the voice again inside his head.

Todd gripped the sides of his head. "Listen we need to talk, Pie. This talking in my mind shit has gotta stop. Can I talk with Pal here and he'll tell you later what we discussed. Is that okay?"

"That would be acceptable," said Pal, his face twisting as if he were angry.

"You don't have to get mad," said Todd easing slowly away from the human shaped alien. He closed his eyes tight. At any moment he expected to be disintegrated by a death ray.

"I'm not mad," replied Pal, his attention returning to the blank wall in front of him, his expression still fixed in a scowl.

"You coulda fooled me." Todd opened his eyes.

"We're nearing the park." The intense concentration on the alien's features amazed Todd. He stood watching the alien manipulate the control panel with a series of deft hand movements. Some resembled karate chops, while others were like palm fronds in a light breeze.

Suddenly he realized they'd stop moving. They'd landed. Now he had to decide how he was going to manage some high-strung FBI types and some aliens, who although they appeared friendly, seemed determined to set their own agenda.

***

This time Pal followed Todd down the ramp to the brown grass of the meadow where the alien ship stood on its tripod landing gear. The grass wasn't green because the city couldn't afford the water to keep in green. The grass would be green for a few weeks in the spring then return to its natural brown, sunburned color in the long, hot days of summer.

At the bottom of the ramp, an excited Guy ran up to him with out-stretched arms. He wrapped him in a bear hug until Pal walked over and lifted Guy away from the startled talk show host. Guy screamed as the alien picked him up, his feet dangled off the ground.

A battery of armored cops appeared with guns drawn, aiming their weapons at Pal. The two FBI agents, who were also armed with automatic pistols, moved into positions on either side of Pal, Todd, and the terrified Guy.

"Guy? I'd like you to meet Pal. He's an alien." Todd signaled to the cops to lower their weapons.

They glanced nervously at each other until Agent Cody spoke in what must be her harshest command voice. "Tell him to put the man down, or I swear to God I'll drop him."

"There's no need for that, Agent Cody."

There was a lump the size of Kansas stuck in Todd's throat as he spoke. His mouth was dry and tasted vaguely metallic. His heart seemed to want to burst between his ribs, it pounded so hard. Sweat ran down from his armpits to tickle the sides of his torso. He caught the scent of garlic from the previous evening's lasagna. He loved the menu and he wondered if he was going to taste any of the fine cuisine ever again after today.

He shook his head as he wiped away the memory. You're not gonna die, Road.

"Pal is not a him," said Todd. "He's an alien who thought I was being attacked. He thinks he's saving me. Isn't that right, Pal?"

Pal gazed at him, his eyes wide, but seemingly uncomprehending. The damn thing was becoming more human with each passing moment. He must realize his error. Surely he'll play along.

Pal nodded then lowered Guy gingerly to the ground and let him go.

Guy scrambled backward and almost fell as he hurried away from the alien, trying to maintain his dignity by pausing to straighten his rumpled suit jacket. His face was flushed and his eyes displayed naked fear.

If I die now, it was worth seeing my boss afraid of something. Maybe the man is human after all.

"Good job, Road," said Guy nervously.

The circle of uniforms moved back while Cody and Williams moved closer, their weapons now pointed at the ground.

"He gonna try anything?" said Williams, eyeing the alien.

Pal stood ramrod straight his lanky arms at his side as he studied his new surroundings. He sniffed the air and wrinkled his nose.

"That's smog," said Todd with a heavy sigh.

He hoped the aliens didn't ask how the air got that way. How would he explain it was humanity's own fault? "Better get used to it. We have lot more where that came from. By the look of the brown air overhead probably gonna be a class three day."

For the past twelve years smog days had been divided into classes. There were classes one through five. Today seemed to be shaping up as a three. Only small animals and old people would die today. Not bad.

"Have you been here before?" asked Todd.

The alien shook his head. "No. I have never been to Earth." His voice sounded warm, almost soft; too gentle, like a child's. Todd felt ill at ease and he didn't know why. What kind of heroic personality did Pie put into this thing?

"So you wanta see my studio?"

The alien smiled again, only this time the corners of his red eyes wrinkled. He was learning.

Todd turned to look at Williams and Cody. "You gonna stop us?"

They shook their heads in unison, their expressions grim. They re-holstered their automatics. "You're calling the shots, Road, for now. But we'll be keeping an eye on you — and your pal," said Cody. They stepped back to let Todd lead the alien toward the waiting limo. Guy followed close behind.

"Do you think this is a good idea?" he whispered in Todd's left ear.

"How many times do you think we'll get to be the first to interview a real alien on my show?" Todd emphasized the word my. He was going to ask for a substantial raise at contract time, and he might as well start softening up Guy right now.

Guy's eyes went wide. "Yeah."

Todd, with a wide show-biz smile on his ruddy face, threw open the door of the limo and swept his free hand like an usher in a theatre. Pal stood and stared at the open door.

"Ever ridden in a chariot before?" Todd asked the bewildered alien.

"It's okay," said Guy reassuringly as he placed his hands on the sides of the alien's shoulders and guided him into the back seat. The alien sat willingly and stared at the two men as they closed the door behind him. They then hurried around the car and got in the other side.

Soon they were speeding through the streets of the city, led by a gauntlet of sky cycle riding cops. The cops cleared the way for them to the speed to the Onyx Corporation building on Regan Boulevard, where the offices of KZAP radio were located.

As they drove along, Pal scanned the world he passed. A mass of people had gathered on the sidewalks to watch the limo pass. Todd saw many of them wearing an earpiece as they listened to live reports from the KZAP studios. He hoped the FBI was monitoring them as well.

The limousine stopped in front of the sixty-story tower in front of the row of glass doors that led into the expansive lobby.

A taxi pulled up behind the limo, and Holly Wodson stepped onto the gray cement of the sidewalk and headed toward them. In her right hand she carried a black, soft-sided briefcase. Her expression was one of annoyance, a deep frown marring her otherwise pleasant appearance. Her short brown hair bounced off her narrow shoulders, and her black heels clicked on the sidewalk as she neared rear door of the limousine.

Todd stepped out the car door and stood next to the car watching her approach with some trepidation.

The woman made him uneasy, though he didn't know why exactly.

"Why did you leave me at the park?" she said angrily when she stood before him.

By this time Guy and Pal were standing just behind Todd. Todd cast Guy a nervous glance. Guy shrugged. He knew that shrug.

It signaled that, since Todd was the radio host who'd made this happen, he would have to take care of it.

He turned to face the enraged lawyer. "We didn't leave you, Ms. Wodson. I didn't know you wanted to come with us."

She snorted. "I thought I made it clear I'm here to protect my client's rights…"

"Sorry. Will you please come with us into my office? It's probably preferable than standing out here on the sidewalk." Todd nodded to the crowd of reporters coming toward them.

"Huh… yes, of course," she said.

Todd smiled briefly and then went through the glass doors from the sidewalk. They were struck by the scent of the vegetation and the sight of the colorful array of tropical birds that fluttered into the air as they entered the lobby. The mixture of sights, smells, and sounds hit them as they left the smoggy city environment behind them.

The temperature in the lobby was considerably warmer, more humid, and tropical than it was outdoors — a change that

could be uncomfortable for the uninitiated.

When Pal was inside he stopped and looked around in wonderment. He raised one arm to stare wide-eyed at the sudden appearance of a perspiration stain in the armpit of his coverall. His mouth formed an 'O'. He gazed wide-eyed at Todd, clearly amazed by the most recent human experience. Didn't they sweat on his world?

Todd wanted to laugh, but held himself back.

Guy's grin was wide, and Todd thought the old man might have broken something for a second.

"This is an artificial environment," said Todd to the puzzled alien. Where he came from, judging by the bland appearance of the vessel in orbit, Pal had probably never seen plants or animals. Todd wondered how they would react to all the life forms on Earth.

Pal nodded then followed them to the bank of elevators. There were fifty elevators on this side of the building.

A lobby security guard was holding a car for them. The group boarded and the doors closed. They rode in silence to the seventeenth floor.

On the way up, Todd was trying to think of a great opening question when they got on the air when it dawned on him. He grinned at Guy whose brow wrinkled.

When the elevator car stopped and the doors slid noiselessly open, they exited into the hallway. They made their way past three closed doors until they came to the door with the word STUDIO in bold black print stenciled on it.

"We'll go right in here," said Todd warmly. Pal nodded. Todd led the way into the producer's booth through the open door. Pal followed him in, and Guy stood aside to let Ms. Wodson enter first. She nodded politely and he smiled thinly.

The smiles disappeared when they were inside. One of the young reporters was on air attempting to fill the void with his views on the events taking place around the world to celebrate the arrival of the aliens.

Amy swiveled her chair as Todd came up behind her. She wore her favorite scarlet knit sweater and blue jeans today. The arms of the sweater were bunched up to reveal the slender white skin of her arms.

Her expression changed to a look of fear when she saw Pal, who was busy studying everything around him as if he were a kid on a school outing.

"Amy," said Todd, after he placed a comforting hand on her right shoulder. She looked up at him from her chair with watery eyes.

The other day she confessed her fear that the alien's arrival foretold the end of the world, and she didn't want her young life to be over before it started. Todd imagined a lot of people were also afraid, Amy's fear was a normal reaction.

"It's okay. I'd like you to meet, Pal." He stepped aside to introduce Pal, who was standing behind him.

Amy stood and reached out with her right hand to shake Pal's hand. Pal smiled warmly at her but kept his hands at his sides.

Amy gave Todd a worried glance. Todd chuckled. Until now he hadn't realized the aliens didn't shake hands as humans did. He hadn't even tried to shake hands when he was on their ship. Of course, the Pel'Tak he'd met hadn't hands to shake with. And until they'd landed 'ol Pal here had been pretty much a robot-man.

"They don't know human customs yet, but they're learning," explained Todd. Amy dropped her hand to her side and smiled nervously at the alien.

"Oh, we know about hand shakes," said Pal. "We just don't like to be in physical contact with other beings. You might have germs, and we don't want to chance breaking our protective seal and carrying some deadly virus back to our home planet."

The four humans glanced at each other, their expressions revealing their uncertainty about meeting an alien.

Protective seal? In a way it made sense.

When astronauts were first sent to the moon, an airless world, they'd been isolated in decontamination chambers after they came back to ensure the safety of the rest of humanity, in case they had been contaminated by deadly space germs. In retrospect it seemed rather silly, but Todd agreed with the idea — it was better to be careful than dead from space germs.

"Makes sense, Pal; how about we go into the studio and talk?"

Pal eyed the reporter through the glass wall, his red eyes brimming with curiosity. "What about him? He seems to be talking to himself. Are you sure it's safe?"

Todd grinned. "Yeah, it's safe. He's on the air right now, and he's about to break for a commercial. We'll go in then."

As the on-air light over the glass wall blinked off, Todd opened the door to the studio. He and Pal went in, while Guy, Amy, and Holly stayed in the booth.

The studio was large enough to hold a large board room table designed to seat twelve. In the center of the room was the control console, with a desk that extended two or three feet from the control board. The desk was kidney-shaped, so the host could reach the controls, and still have space for documents, or other materials he might need to have handy.

A sleek silver microphone and two white plastic ear pieces were ready for them to use. Todd explained to Pal that the right one was placed in his ear it allowed him to hear his producer offering instructions or suggestions, while the other let him hear the guest or link callers who called into the show to offer their opinions.

There were several low-backed chairs resting on their plastic casters on the other side of the desk from where Todd sat. He indicated to Pal he should sit on one, which the alien did.

Todd had to get over that the person seated across from him was a real alien. The alien had a name, so he was a person, just as a Chinese or a Russian was a person. He was just from a place a little farther away than either of those nationalities.

He glanced at Amy who held up four fingers. They were about to go on the air. His armpits grew moist and the room seemed suddenly filled with his own Burma-Shave-scented sweat. He tried to clear his throat and realized his throat was dry. He licked his lips and the taste of bile came up from the back of his mouth.

This was the biggest day of his career. He would have not just a national audience but a worldwide audience. He could hardly comprehend how famous he was about to become.

With trembling fingers he placed the dual earpieces in his ears just as the on-air light lit up. He glanced at the time indicator on his board: 10:34.

"We're back. Thanks, Sergio, for that excellent report. This is Todd Road and we're on the road." Todd paused while Amy cued his theme song, the old Willie Nelson tune, On the Road Again. One he'd loved since he was a child.

The music gradually dropped off until there was silence in his twin earpieces. This was the moment when he'd make history instead of just being part of it. The first broadcast conversation with a being from another star, another planet. And it was his program. On the Road with Todd Road was about to go where no radio show had gone before.

He was suddenly overwhelmed by a feeling of giddiness he'd not felt since he was a kid gazing at the bright packages under the Yule tree.

"Ladies and gentlemen, this is a big day for the program." He paused for dramatic effect.

"Today we introduce to you, the American public, coast-to-coast, Pal — an alien from another planet who is here to visit us humble Earth dwellers. Say hello, my friend."

Pal sat watching him, his hands resting in his lap. Todd couldn't read his expression so he had no idea how the Vel'Tan would react. "Hello," Pal said politely.

"For the clarification of our audience perhaps you could explain who you are and where you come from."

Todd was stretching it, holding his breath, waiting for Pal to speak. It was entirely possible that Pal might not choose to say anything and the audience may think his broadcast was a hoax, some science fiction special effects thing. He wished Pal didn't look or sound so darned human.

"Certainly, Todd, I'd be happy to," said Pal after only a moment's hesitation. "I'm from a race of people called the Vel'Tan. We come from a star in what I believe your astronomers call Orion's belt. We are symbiots with a species known as the Pel'Tak. We are humanoid in appearance while our symbiotic counterparts are not.

"The Pel'Tak live suspended in a fluid and are composed of electrically charged filaments. We are the builders while the Pel'Tak are the thinkers, diplomats, and scientists." Pal stopped to smile at Todd knowingly. "They have evolved beyond the ability to do physical labor. We fill that need. We serve them while they provide us with organic bodies and food and shelter. The Pel'Tak and Vel'Tan live in perfect balance."

Todd was startled to realize Pal was aware the people listening couldn't see him, this required he describe things in more detail so people listening understood.

Todd thought for a second maybe the alien could transmit its thoughts like the Pel'Tak, but immediately dismissed the idea. So far, Pal had not shown any sign of having that ability.

"Thank you, Pal." Todd smiled and nodded to indicate Pal had done well.

"Let's get to the heart of the matter, shall we?" Todd paused for dramatic effect. "Why are you here? Exactly."

Todd looked into those unemotional red eyes and saw them darken. Pal's facial features were suddenly hard and Todd knew immediately he'd pressed some button he probably shouldn't have. Then Pal's features softened.

"I have been briefed on your customs and practices prior to my mission; however, I know human law is controversial, so maybe I'd better save my comments for another time."

Todd took a deep breath. He was going for broke. "Pal, Mike Sikes said on this program, that you and the Pel'Tak are here to free him. You claim he's innocent. I want to understand how you know this with such certainty when all evidence points to the contrary."

Pal sighed heavily. For the first time his red gaze dropped to the floor. There was several seconds of silence, during which Todd felt the trickle of perspiration running down the inside of his shirt from his armpits.

"Todd," said Amy in his ear piece.

He glanced over and saw her pointing frantically at a very agitated Holly Wodson with her arms crossed in front of her and her face flushed. "She wants to talk to you right now."

What the hell? He was in the middle of his program, his career topping interview. He glared at Amy, but she pointed at Wodson again and growled in his earpiece that it was important

“Sorry, ladies and gentlemen. Before Pal answers my question we have some business to conduct. We still have to pay the bills around here.” Todd chuckled. “We’ll be right back after these words from our sponsors.”

He cut his microphone and pulled the ear pieces out of his ears and laid them on the smooth, cool surface of the desk.

Pal looked at him, his eyes steady and calm. Todd smiled to assure him, hoping the alien wasn’t annoyed at the interruption. “I’ll be right back,” he said to the alien, who nodded.

Todd hurried into the control booth and closed the door behind him so Pal wouldn’t hear what they were saying.

“What the fuck are you doing, Mr. Road?” said Holly Wodson between gritted teeth.

“I’m interviewing my guest. What does it look like?”

Amy was busy with her board to ensure there was no dead air. She would have to run more than one segment of commercials. This unscheduled break would take some time to sort out.

“It looks like you’re jeopardizing my client’s defense. The aliens are his chance to prove his innocence. What they have to say should be heard first in a court of law. Mike deserves the best defense. After that I don’t care what you do with these things.”

Anger flared in Todd, he sneered. “Defense? What defense? The son of a bitch killed people. He has no defense for that.”

Holly shifted her weight to her right side and glared at him. “I thought you were on his side?”

“Mike’s side? Where did you get an idea like that?”

Holly nodded toward the alien sitting in his studio gazing about the room, taking everything in. When he saw Todd looking at him he smiled and waved. Todd grinned then faced Holly.

"Listen, that's show business. Ratings. I never actually said I believed Mike. I may have led Mike and them…" he indicated Pal with a slight nod, "...astray, but so what? Life is a bitch, what can I say?"

Holly rolled her eyes and dropped her hands to her side. "You bastard, do you have any idea what you've done?"

"Good radio, fantastic ratings," Todd said with pride in his voice.

Holly shook her head. "You've created an interstellar incident. One which may be the death of us all."

"What?" It was Amy who'd swiveled her low-backed chair to face the two invaders in her space.

Todd waved Amy off.

"How do you think they'd feel if they discovered the one person on the planet who Mike Sikes trusted was revealed as a liar. That in fact he didn't believe them or Mike?"

Todd hesitated. Wodson might be right. His cheeks grew cold. Yeah, how would they react? Death rays, alien torture chambers, slave camps — any manner of punishment his fertile mind could dream up was probably already in their inventory of alien horrors.

"Oh, crap," he said in a low voice.

SEVEN

THE ON-AIR LIGHT CAME ON as soon as Todd settled into his studio chair. Amy, sitting in her booth watching him, her face pale and her eyes fearful, signaled that he was on. Behind her stood Holly, whose brow was wrinkled by worry.

He cleared his throat. “Ladies and gentlemen of my esteemed audience. I’ve been advised by the KZAP legal department that I must refrain from delving into Mike Sikes’s guilt or innocence for the remainder of our interview with Pal. I urge you, my beloved audience to also refrain from asking questions along this line. I would not wish to offend long-time listeners by having to disconnect them.

“I know this is contrary to the higher moral ground I usually adhere to on this program, but believe me, it is necessary in this instance.”

He paused to glance at Holly who nodded grimly.

Damn her, he thought.

“What I will guarantee you, my friends, is this: before this is over, we will have the answers we seek.” He stole a glance at Holly whose arms were thrown in the air over her head as she berated Amy with a verbal deluge.

"She's not happy." He heard Amy say in a low voice into his ear. He smiled to himself.

"Now, Pal, let's talk about why you're here and what you hope to accomplish while here on Earth. Are you going to play tourist, see the sights?" Todd smiled.

"No, Mr. Road, we are not here to visit, as you put it; we are here to save our species from extinction."

Todd started, this was a new development. "Please explain," he said leaning forward to rest his arms on the table's smooth surface.

The alien smiled and warmed to his subject.

He explained that on his home world, the Vel'Tan were becoming extinct. Current projections were that they would disappear within two to five hundred Earth years.

The Pel'Tak, seeking a solution, since they were would continue for several hundred years without the Vel'Tan, began to search the galaxy in earnest for a substitute species to take the place of their dying symbiots.

"Do you mean to take some of us to your planet as symbiots for the Pel'Tak? Is that why you're here?"

Pal laughed brightly, and the corners of his eyes wrinkled. He was really getting into this human thing. "Oh, no, Mr. Road. All we need is a DNA sample from the right human to clone our new race. Mike Sikes is that human."

EIGHT

Mike Sikes slept very little during the night. He tossed and turned on the lumpy prison mattress. The guards had no doubt given him the lumpiest mattress they could find. With the seemingly endless bumps and sharp springs pressing against his spine every night, the bedding did its job in making him too tired to think straight.

Not that he expected anything different, the lumpy mattress he'd spent his formative years sleeping on at his mother's home was much the same as this one. Abuse was his middle name.

He shaved at his usual time, and the large black guard delivered his breakfast to his cell at the appointed hour of 8:00 a.m., just as he did every day. The guard served his usual side of disgust, as if Mike were a waste of space and his time. Mike's eyes narrowed and his mouth formed a lopsided, humorless grin that made the guard look uncertain for the first time since he had been locked up.

It was because Mike Sikes was now the most important person on Earth.

Today the aliens were going to come here and break him out of his confinement.

Maybe they'd use one of those alien ray guns he'd read about in a pulp SF novel when he was a kid. More likely, they'd use their minds to remove the walls and the bars.

Pie had been able to use his mental abilities to contact him, so why couldn't they remove a few simple inanimate objects such as bars and walls?

At 8:30 Mike zipped up his gray prison coverall over his white sleeveless undershirt. He pushed the button on the wall next to the sink, and the sink disappeared into a slot in the wall.

He turned back to his bunk and sipped the last of his tepid, milky coffee as the guard appeared through the view port in the steel door.

"You got visitors, Sikes." It was the blond meat-head.

Mike nodded, then adjusted his narrow shoulders to make himself appear bigger than he actually was, stood, and walked to the door, his chin held high.

The metal scraping across the concrete floor echoed in his ears as he passed through the open door. The two burly guards stood with his restraints at the ready. They carried both leg and arms restraints this time. This was a special circumstance, which Warden Carter said meant they would revert to their standard policy of maximum restraint for dangerous prisoners, such as him.

He stood still as the guards applied the rubberized ankle and wrist shackles, then engaged the automated security system. The restraints tightened enough so that he could walk without too much difficulty. Of course, if he tried to run, or make any unauthorized movements, the restraints would tighten until he fell over, immobilized. He'd be trussed up like a calf being roped in the pictures of the old rodeos he'd seen at the museum when he was a kid.

He smiled at the guards who nodded grimly to each other. The prisoner was ready for transport.

Three men, the smaller one in the middle, started down the corridor, their footsteps echoing off the cement and steel walls toward the visiting room.

The room would again be empty today, expect for the guards, the visitors, and the prisoner. Mingling wasn't allowed when Mike had visitors, because of the risk that the other prisoners or their families, including their children, might be planning to kill Mike if anyone got close enough to him.

A portable electronic security grid had been installed around the prisoner visiting room today as a precaution. The only weapons permitted were the ones carried by the guards.

They entered the room to find Holly, a very sweaty fat man that had to be Todd Road, and the red-eyed alien waiting for him. They were spread around the room, standing apart as if they were strangers waiting at a sky bus terminal.

Mike's pale, hairless features broke into a maniacal grin when he saw the assembled group waiting for humanity's star of the hour.

He'd hoped the press would be present at such a momentous occasion. From the corner of his eye Mike spotted Hamilton, his hands folded in front of him, standing in the shadows at the end of the room.

The son of a bitch was smiling as he watched the assembly. He was probably smiling because he'd managed to keep the press corps outside. Smug. One day he'd wipe that smile off the man's face.

Mike's eyes narrowed momentarily, then he reverted to his best glad-to-meet-ya smile and tried to throw his arms wide in greeting. But the restraints reacted by becoming tighter making movement impossible, and causing him considerable pain.

Thankfully he hadn't tried to run, or he'd be lying on his face on the floor with a broken nose, a bad headache, and hands and feet with no circulation for a week. The guards would have enjoyed that.

He watched them glance at each other and smirk at his discomfort.

"Damn, these things," he said aloud which caused the knot of visitors stare at him.

He moved to the center of the room his arms held in front of him. One guard nodded and ordered the restraints to loosen their grip. Reluctantly he glanced at Hamilton who nodded his approval.

"Holly, it's so good to see you. And you, too, Mr. Road. I feel that I know you somehow better than anyone I've ever actually met."

Todd stepped forward with his best I-wanna-be-in-pictures smile, took Mike's offered hand in his, and shook it warmly, slapping Mike on the back with the other hand. Out of the corner of his eye, Mike saw the guards tense. He smiled to himself.

"It's nice to finally meet you, Mike," said Todd.

Mike could see in Todd's eyes he wasn't telling the whole truth. His internal caution light came on. Mike was determined not to reveal his true feelings toward this man — his instincts had saved his butt more times than he could count. The one time they'd failed him, he'd ended up on death row. He wouldn't let this happen ever again.

"And you, Mr. Road. Listen I was wondering if you could get these Nazi's to remove the these things completely?" Mike held up his hands to show the blue rubberized restraints and moved one leg causing the chain linking them together to rattle.

Todd glanced at Holly with concern in his eyes. Not that Mike cared. For her part Holly shrugged the radio host off.

Mike smiled to himself. The smarmy devil wasn't getting help from her.

Todd next eyed the warden standing now nearer to the group. His gatekeeper nodded to the guards who gave each other a worried expression and hesitated.

The warden frowned and nodded strongly at them to indicate his displeasure. One of the guards moved forward and removed the ankle restraints then backed away with the restraints in his meaty hands.

Mike smiled to himself. The guards are scared, and he loved it.

"And the other set too," said Carter in a low voice.

The other guard came up to Mike keeping his inky black gaze fixed on Mike's. The pure hate in his gaze shot through the serial killer as if he was willing the smaller man to try something. He removed the wrist restraints.

Both guards had one meaty hand resting on the butt of their holstered side arms. The strap that held the weapon from being drawn was unbuttoned for a quick release. Their foreheads were wrinkled by intensity.

They stood back and watched Mike carefully ready to fill his body with lead if he tried any unauthorized moves.

Holly Wodson appeared nervous, her hands were trembling.

Not that they had anything to worry about.

The visitor's room was forty seven stories above the ground. Even if a prisoner tried to escape via the room's skylight windows, the fall would turn him into jam when he hit the ground. That was only if the high winds that buffeted the walls didn't smash the-would-be escape artist to a pulp against the tower on the way down. Escape was not an option.

Mike smiled at the guards, then turned his attention to the alien who had been watching this drama unfold with an expression of mild amusement.

The alien stepped forward and held out one pale, pinkish hand. "Hello, Mr. Sikes. My name is Pal. I'm here to free you. You have been wrongly incarcerated."

The silence of the next several seconds filled the room with tension so thick it felt like a foggy morning on a San Francisco harbor. There was the sound of the wind hitting the skylight windows some twenty-five feet above their heads.

Now the alien was going to ask the government to release one of the worst mass killers in history. Prison prisoner alpha, six three two seven, slash B, Mike Sikes was free.

"Pal, we are prepared to meet your terms and conditions," said Carter, his expression grim.

"What do you mean?" he said to Carter, his gaze calm but narrow with suspicion.

"Mike, you know we can't just release you without careful planning. You know what would happen — you have more enemies outside these walls than inside."

Mike nodded. "You know you're right, Ham. Maybe I'd be safer under the care of these aliens."

Mike nodded toward the red-eyed alien, who continued to smile warmly. Pal said nothing. It seemed all he wanted to do for now was observe.

"Ms. Wodson. What's going on here?" said Todd, glancing back and forth between the Warden and Sikes.

"I don't know," said Holly with a puzzled expression her face.

"I'll explain. Mr. Sikes is to be released into the supervision of the alien, his lawyer, and Mr. Todd Road by order of the President of the United States," Carter said, reading from a data pad he'd pulled from his inside suit pocket.

Mike, who'd seen many of the Warden's suits, noticed that he'd worn his beloved blue pinstripe (the one with the stylish, wide lapels, and his favorite maroon-colored shirt). Hamilton had never said these were his favorites, but since he only wore them on special occasions, Mike suspected they were. He'd been trying for months to confirm this theory without success.

The look of revulsion mingled with anger on their faces told him Road and Wodson had no idea of this decision. How he loved the politicians, they spring so much crap on you at the last minute. They were speechless.

He reveled at being right. It was the only thing in life that ever mattered to him. Being wrong was unacceptable, and to him a sign of moral weakness; those who were wrong deserved to die. And liars were even worse. He'd planned many a painful and prolonged death for them. He eyed Todd who was busy whispering to a very worried-looking Holly Wodson.

"So, Pal, my good, new, friend—my friend from the stars. When do you think we should get outta here?" said Mike.

"How's about we go to my studio first and have an interview to mark the occasion of your freedom. The first time you have breathed free air in…?"

Mike couldn't help but admire this bald weasel, in his five-thousand dollar designer suit and expensive Italian leather shoes, clothes worth more than a month's pay to average slob on the street. He was one hell of a showman. PT Barnum would have been proud.

Mike nodded. "Yeah, I think that would be great. What about you, Pal?" The alien smiled and nodded, his red gaze focused on Mike's.

***

Mike, Todd, Holly, and Pal, flanked by heavily-armed police guards, arrived at the Onyx Corporation building to find a mob of protesters being held back by a heavily-armed contingent of police dressed in riot gear.

The mob was comprised of people of every age group and social strata; grandmothers, school children, teenagers, and men in business suits carrying brief cases, all of whom waved homemade placards to vent their displeasure with the release of Mike Sikes.

The words painted on the signs said it all.

Baby killer!

Monster!

Son of Hitler!

Kill the Killer!

Some of the crowd screamed obscenities at them as they stepped onto the sidewalk.

They were flanked by police, who were attempting to restraint the enraged and screaming mob behind hastily-erected energy barriers.

A white-faced Todd Road stared at the seething mass of humanity. He watched a gray-haired woman fall to the ground where she lay still, her eyes wide as she was overcome by the electric shocks emitted by the barrier. The barriers weren't meant to kill, but she was old, probably weakened by the combination of the crushing mob, the loss of available oxygen, and the energy from the barrier.

Todd could see one of the senior cops, with four gold stripes on the left sleeve of his black uniform, frantically wrestling with the barrier controller as it sparked furiously, threatening to overload in some sections.

Golden sparks danced in the air as the mob pressed against the barrier. The mob would overload the system soon, and the barrier would fail.

Then the cops would have their hands full to contain these people.

"We better get inside," said Todd, his voice steady. He certainly didn't feel steady.

They moved into the lobby, where uniformed Onyx security guards locked steel bars across the front doors behind them. No doubt the fire marshal would have a field day with this breach of regulations, but they couldn't let the mob invade the building. Todd knew if they got inside they'd rip Mike limb from limb. Not a bad thing really, but right now he was useful to the world, and to him.

"I don't think they understand," said Pal.

"You got that right," said Holly, her expression grim. Mike eyed her.

They crossed the marble-covered lobby to the bank of elevators.

Once they reached the seventeenth floor, they went down the familiar hall to the studio. As they entered, Todd caught Amy's frightened expression. The girl was an open book. He smiled briefly and nodded to her.

Yamata was in the studio, giving a report on the mob at the ground floor of the Onyx tower. When he saw Todd enter the room followed by his entourage, he cued-up a commercial for a local organ replication big-box outlet with monster sales and a budget to match, as compared with the mom and pop shops with no advertising budget, and leapt from his chair.

This time Holly entered the studio with Todd. She'd made it clear she didn't care for him, and she wasn't about to let him incriminate her client on the air, as he'd done so often in the past.

Todd sat behind his desk in front of the control board while Pal, Mike, and Holly sat in the chairs on the opposite side of the desk.

They sat unmoving while Todd waited for the commercial Yamata had started to finish, Yamata smiled, thin-lipped at Todd then turned and fled the room, not bothering to glance back as he hurried out of the studio.

The look on his young face was one of pure terror.

The jingle ended. Todd smiled at a somber Holly and the grinning serial killer beside her. Pal appeared relaxed and comfortable, even having crossed his legs and folded his thin hands in his lap. His red eyes betrayed nothing other than he was at peace.

Todd envied the alien his calm demeanor. His stomach was so knotted he thought he'd puke any second.

From the control room, Amy cued the theme song.

As it began to fade Todd began. "This is Todd Road and we're on the road."

The music swelled briefly then again died. In the silence Todd paused for effect then began to speak.

"Ladies and gentlemen of the listening audience I am here with Pal, the alien visitor you have all become so familiar with, and Mike Sikes, live in our studio. Also with us today is Holly Wodson, Mike's legal counsel."

Todd chuckled. "For reasons that escape me, Ms. Wodson thinks I said something inappropriate to our alien visitor the last time he was on our show. Perhaps we'll begin by exploring that issue."

Holly shot daggers at him as he cast his gaze toward the red-faced lawyer. He was baiting her in an attempt to embarrass her into either leaving them alone in the studio, or better yet, saying something really stupid over an open mike.

"Ms. Wodson, how are you today?"

"Fine," she said in a low voice.

He tapped the side of his head above his right ear. "Sorry, Ms. Wodson, can you speak up, please?"

"Yes, I can," she said louder.

Her left eye winced slightly. "So, Ms. Wodson, please explain to our listening audience why…"

"Cut the crap, Road." Mike interrupted. His brow was wrinkled and his eyes narrow. Todd's heart began to beat faster. "Let's get to the real reason I'm here."

Todd's expression briefly betrayed his disappointment. He would have enjoyed tearing this smug bitch a new one, but that would have to wait. Then he brightened and turned his attention to Mike Sikes, sitting with his lanky arms folded in his lap and his legs crossed.

"Of course; sorry, Mike. Let's talk about you."

Mike smiled.

How the asshole loves the spot light. "What are your plans, now that you've met Pal?"

Mike gazed at him, his eyes suddenly wide. Todd could tell the arrogant son of a bitch had no idea. Damn. Was this any way to run a talk show?

Faced with dead air, Todd shifted his focus. "Pal, what are your next steps?"

"To prove Mr. Sikes's innocence," said the affable alien.

"So you think he's innocent?"

"Undoubtedly." Pal shrugged, as if Mike's innocence were a well-established fact.

Todd frowned.

"How can you be so certain?" asked Todd. He was genuinely curious. He'd played the innocence game for months, but he never really believed.

Since their last discussion on this topic, one in which he'd not gotten an answer to this all important question, he and his valued listening audience, wanted a concrete reason to this question. Thus far he'd yet to hear anything from these aliens to convince him Mike Sikes wasn't the monster everyone thought he was.

Pal's expression remained unflappable as he calmly responded, "He does not have the mental capacity to commit the crimes."

That was when all hell broke loose in the studios of KZAP radio.

NINE

TODD THOUGHT HE HEARD MUSIC — a jingle, for a funeral service company. Maybe he was dead? Is that was what happens to you when you die? The angels play funeral music for you?

He slowly opened his eyes. Through blurred vision, and a throbbing head, he managed to make out the gray ceiling of his studio.

He recognized it because several months ago Guy had the art department paint a logo for Todd's show in the center of the gray expanse. He was gazing at a picture of himself dressed in his tan suit and tie, and seated in an old fashioned convertible automobile. Only a few such cars still existed in the hands of collectors.

His image was smiling with one thumb pointed up. Underneath his picture, in bright red, highly stylized letters were the words, You're On the Road with Todd Road.

He wasn't dead. He took in a deep breath and realized his chest hurt. He sat up with one hand flat on his chest.

It was then he noticed two high heeled woman's shoes peeking from behind the desk.

Todd managed to struggle to his knees, his breath coming in gasps.

The pain in his chest reminded him of someone sitting on his chest. His eyes watered. He blinked rapidly and managed to clear his vision.

He tried to take in another deep breath. It came easier this time, but still hurt.

Finally he crawled on his hands and knees to check on the wearer of the shoes and discovered Holly lying on her side.

Her arms were askew, and when he managed to get beside her he saw her eyes were open. Her neck was twisted at an unnatural angle.

Taking her right wrist in his fingers he checked for a pulse. Finding none he touched her forehead and realized her skin was cold. Holly was dead — and had been for a while.

Scanning the room he realized Mike and Pal were gone. He was alone with a dead lawyer. Where's Amy? His pulse quickened and he ran his tongue over his dry lips. He had to find her.

Raising himself to his knees he ignored the pain running the length of his body until he finally managed to pull himself to his feet, steadying himself by holding onto the desk. For a moment, he bent over with his eyes closed to clear his head. Dizziness and nausea threatened to overwhelm him. His stomach churned and he swallowed sour bile rising in the back of his throat.

He stumbled to the door to the control room and leaned against the wall with his eyes shut. Taking in another deep breath, he then slowly exhaled through his mouth. His breath sounded ragged to his ears.

Beads of perspiration broke out on his forehead. Was it excessively hot in here, or was his imagination playing tricks on him?

The room moved about him as if he were a drunken sailor. Though intellectually he knew it wasn't moving at all.

He winced then reached up to the top of his bald head with his right hand, and felt something damp on his fingertips. He pulled back his fingers and gazed at them. They were red. He was bleeding. He'd been wounded before, so blood didn't bother him as long as the wound wasn't fatal. And he hoped he'd survive this one.

How long had it been since....he couldn't seem to recall...

With pain shooting down his side and a throbbing head, he managed to turn the door handle to the control room and stumble through.

Amy was lying on her back, her eyes closed. Todd's heart skipped a beat until he noticed her chest moving with each shallow breath. There wasn't any blood in evidence. She was alive, but out cold. Tears welled in his eyes. He'd grown very fond of Amy; if she died because of his ambition, he'd never forgive himself.

He stood then collapsed in her swiveled chair next to her prone body. He needed to call someone...the FBI agents...Williams and Cody, where were they any way? They must have been near the prison and somewhere nearby the station.

Dizziness gripped him. The room began to whirl about him. He closed his eyes and gripped the chair arms. The odor of his own sour, salty sweat enveloped him.

The door to the hallway behind him burst open. He opened one eye, and through a haze of pain agent saw Angela Cody, framed in the doorway, her gun held out before her, scanning for targets.

She froze when she saw Todd. Then her eyes drifted to Amy, lying unmoving on the floor.

The world began to spin; blackness engulfed him. Todd needed sleep.

Agent Cody and the rest of the world disappeared into a dark abyss.

***

When Todd opened his eyes again, he winced from the sudden rush of bright light.

There was a slight pinch in his right arm, and he realized he was attached to an intravenous drip attached to a metal stand next to the bed. He was in a hospital room.

He ran a hand over his head only to discover it wrapped in a bandage. Pulling back the bed covers, he found himself dressed in a white hospital gown and nothing else.

He flushed when he realized someone, probably a nurse, had undressed him. Not that he was a modest man, but he didn't like the idea of some stranger touching him when he wasn't awake. He wasn't a prude, but nudity was best reserved for bedtime hours when two people were alone.

Instinctively he ran his right hand up and down his body. Oddly his left hand wouldn't move. To his relief everything seemed to be intact, right where it should be, except his left arm didn't work. Sikes had been known to take souvenirs from his victims. Except he wasn't a victim. He was still alive. Why?

As he puzzled over this the door to his room opened to reveal a frowning Amy.

Her face sported a nasty, purplish bruise on the left cheek and a brownish-red bandage over the right eye, The flesh around the patch was swollen and surrounded with ugly purple bruises.

When she saw he was awake, tears began to flow down her cheeks. She rushed to his bedside and grasped his right hand in both of her slim hands.

He smiled weakly. “Amy,” he sighed. “It’s good to see you’re okay.”

Her voice cracked as she spoke. “Todd, I’m sorry....”

“What....?”

“Wodson is dead and ... ”

He tugged his arm and the chain attached to the steel handcuff around his left wrist rattled against the stainless steel rail. He eyed the polished bar running the length of his hospital bed. “I’m being blamed aren’t I?”

She nodded.

“Where’s Williams and Cody?”

“I —”

Before Amy could say more, they were interrupted by Agent Cody who burst into the room. Her navy suit jacket waved about her, and her shoulder-length hair bobbed against her shoulders. The woman was a force of nature. He was pretty sure she wasn’t entirely human.

“Agent Williams is dead,” she said approaching his bedside.

Todd gazed at her and mouthed the word ‘really?’ to Amy who nodded then cast her watery eyes downward, her hand gripping his tighter.

“As you’ve gathered by now, Road you’re under arrest as an accessory to murder. Len Williams, Holly Wodson, Guy Thompson, Clark Yamata...”

Todd was too stunned to speak as she listed off the names of the dead — everyone who worked for KZAP, except him and Amy, and of course, Agent Williams. Also some names of people he didn’t recognize.

This was nuts, it couldn’t be right.

Cody then began to read him his revised constitutional rights. He half listened to the FBI agent drone on.

Mike had wiped out everyone except them. Himself, Amy, and Cody… why?

"Where's Mike, and the alien?" he asked.

Cody ignored him until she'd finished reciting her prepared speech. "We don't know," she said, obviously embarrassed to have to admit this.

How can that be? "But the surveillance sats, the security net… "

"Everything's out of commission."

Todd knew they would have already tried the kill switch to take Mike out. That must have failed as well. His eyeballs became wide with the realization of the ramifications of what Cody was telling him. That meant the son of bitch was on the loose, with no way to stop him.

He shook his head. "That's impossible."

She shrugged her expression grim. "It seems the devices your new friends put in orbit have drained all of the internal power systems of our surveillance and intelligence network, worldwide."

His eyes went wider as the sudden realization dawned on him why she was here. "You need me for something. Don't you?"

Cody turned away, one hand on her hip holding her jacket aside. She stepped away from the bed her back to him. Her proud shoulders slumped a little and he heard her sigh. Without turning around she added, "Yes, Mr. Road, as much as it pains me to say it, we need you. Will you help us?"

"Give me one good reason why I should." He rattled the handcuff chain to emphasize his point. "I've been arrested, for God's sake."

She turned around and faced him, her expression one of frustration.

Amy started and moved closer to the head of the bed, as if she were protecting him.

“Because, Mr. Road, if you don’t, my director is going to make you fry for those deaths. He wants you, Pal, and Mike Sikes to pay. He’s claiming it’s a conspiracy and that you’re the ringleader.”

She paused and her expression softened. “I personally don’t believe that shit. I blame myself.”

“Oh, fuck-off,” said Todd. “You? You had nothing to do with Mike killing those people. I… the guy’s an animal. He likes to kill. Besides how the hell are you going to catch an alien? Frankly, what bothers me is why didn’t he kill the three of us?”

Angela cocked an eyebrow. “Mike…I mean,” Todd clarified.

Todd glanced at Amy who shrugged, then back at Angela. “Tell me something, Agent Cody. How did the others die?”

Angela looked thoughtful. “My partner evacuated everyone to the street while I stayed behind.”

She cast her eyes to the floor and her tone now had a bitter edge. “There was an explosion. The sidewalk, the limousine waiting outside, and anyone within fifty meters, including Len, your co-workers, and fifty protestors, were all vaporized.”

“So that couldn’t have been Mike’s doing now, could it?”

Angela shook her head. “No. My director thinks you told your alien friend, Pal, to kill them. Personally, I don’t think they were behind the explosion. I mean sure Mike probably killed poor Holly himself, but I suspect someone else is responsible for the explosion or whatever it was that took out the others.” She crossed her arms and shrugged. “I think you’re my primo numero uno suspect.”

“But what about the disruption of the surveillance net?” said Amy, expressing out loud what Todd and Angela were thinking. They both looked at her. She shrugged. “What? Did I say something wrong?”

If the aliens were behind the explosion that killed those people, they were also the ones responsible for Holly's death. The problem was, if this was true then the future of the human race looked bleak indeed.

A real war of the worlds might be just around the corner.

TEN

THE GLOWING GLOBE containing the essence of the Pel'Tak known as Pie, floated over the control surface. A force field surrounding it kept the container aloft.

Pie was suffering a deep sadness and regret at the images coming to him from the web globes he'd placed in Lagrange orbits above the planet. The web globes were transmitting images directly into his receptors.

His interstellar ship sat in a high orbit, well beyond the humans' primitive spy satellites. He fully expected they'd try to watch him, but it would take weeks to re-task their satellites and move them to high-enough orbits.

He was shocked when one satellite actually did get close, but he'd quickly scrambled its software, causing it to spin out of orbit crashing into one of Earth's oceans. The humans were a clever species. Maybe too clever.

He sensed time was growing short, but he anticipated his job would be long over before the humans could interfere with any effectiveness.

It was unfortunate that he'd been forced to interfere with the human's surveillance systems, but they would have harmed the savior, and that was unacceptable. Interference with another species was distasteful to the Pel'Tak.

The Order had also instructed him to lie, which was equally distasteful, but necessary for the survival of their race.

The web globe orbiting the planet showed him the escape of his operative and the savior just before the explosion. The explosion wasn't planned, but it had to be; he had to save Mike Sikes. Nothing else mattered. Humans died, but it couldn't be helped. It pained him to have to take life, any life. It wasn't the Pel'Tak way — but they hoped it would be, some day.

The savior had instructed him not to read his thoughts, so he was forced to comply. The savior's instructions were not to be disobeyed under any circumstances. The Order had been quite clear on this.

He moved to the interface and contacted Pal. The savior did not forbid contact with his operative.

Are you well?

For the moment, came the immediate reply.

For the first time in his long life Pie felt fear. A cold wave of it entered his being. It was coming from Pal. This feeling was a foreign concept and one which he didn't enjoy. How did humans live with this? His race would have gone mad with the paralysis fear caused in him.

Pie swept the feeling from his conscious thoughts utilizing techniques taught by the Order.

Where are you going? Pie asked.

I'm with the savior and we are on our way to prove his innocence, Pal replied.

Pie was relieved. The mission had not been compromised. In spite of his newly acquired human failing, fear, Pal would complete his task. The Vel'Tan would accompany Mike to various locations on Earth and prove he was the true savoir of their race. Good.

He would relay a message home. The Order would be pleased with his progress.

The savior would fulfill his destiny, just as it was foretold in the ancient texts, written when the Pel'Tak walked about on two appendages on their world as these beings did, in the time before the great awakening, the prophecy describing the renewal process of their species. .

Mike Sikes would be the first to join the new Order to be established here, on Earth. The humans would experience the awakening, and would join with the Pel'Tak. They would continue, together, toward the time of perfection, toward the ascension.

The time of the Vel'Tan was fast ending. As it was foretold, the Pel'Tak must evolve to survive. And the only way to evolve was to learn to kill —Mike Sikes would teach them. And then he would die as an example to their race. A vision of their future.

ELEVEN

Mike studied Pal sitting behind the ship's control panel. He was staring at what looked to Mike like a blank, shimmering wall of gelatin.

Pal had put on a highly stylized headset when they'd gotten on board. The headset consisted of a thin, plastic strap that ran around his head with two opaque lenses in front of his red eyes. These distorted his eyes into misshapen portals and caused the pupils to change color intermittently. Sometimes red, sometimes green, and sometimes blue.

Mike had to admit he was fascinated by the alien's ability to pilot the craft. He didn't feel any movement, though they were probably traveling faster than even the most advanced aircraft currently in military service.

These beings had a lot to teach the human race. He swelled with pride every time he thought about his contribution in bringing them here.

Several prominent physicists who had appeared on Todd's show said the alien craft didn't break the sound barrier, even at supersonic speeds, though the eggheads didn't know how it was possible for the craft go faster than any Earth-bound aircraft, and they were unwilling to embarrass themselves by speculating. He smirked. The aliens' ship simply bent time, a warp in the time space continuum making it possible for them to appear to outpace human aircraft. It was obvious.

They all thought they were so fucking smart. Even Holly Wodson thought she was smarter than him. He'd shown her just how smart he was in the end, hadn't he?

"We'll be at our destination in two of your minutes," said Pal, still focused on the wall in front of him. Mike narrowed his eyes to gaze at the blank featureless surface.

Mike nodded. Surely Pal, being an alien and all, knew what he was doing. After all, the aliens were at least as smart as him.

***

They exited the ship via a ramp, probably the same one he'd seen Pal and Todd use at the park in the city.

Pal assured Mike that they'd not been tracked. His friends in the mother ship had already disabled the worldwide surveillance net. The ident chips implanted in every person when they were born would be useless except to hand scanners. And the cops couldn't scan everyone.

He breathed deeply to take in the country air. The pig farm was just as he remembered it — the smell of pig feces as strong as ever.

The log house, surrounded by chain-linked fences and the pens that used to hold hundreds of hungry pigs were where he remembered them.

He'd disposed of bodies here. He fed them to the pigs.

The lying FBI investigators said they'd found DNA of the victims in the mud-covered ground. Mike knew it was all part a government conspiracy to frame him. Regardless of the fact that he had killed those women, they would never have been able to prove any of their allegations without framing him.

The FBI, the ATF, and the CIA manufactured evidence to silence dissents like him, who rejected the technological world built by the government, and its agents. Don't upset the status quo or they'll make you pay.

He walked across the dirt lot toward the rough-hewn house. Pal followed close behind him down the ramp. They marched toward the darkened house. The wooden-planked floorboards creaked as Mike mounted the porch. The screen door's rusty hinges squealed loudly as he pulled the door open.

Cobwebs greeted him when he went inside. The last of daylight was streaming in through dirt-covered windows, casting a rainbow of color near the edges of his vision.

He glanced about the room trying to find it. He knew it had to be here somewhere. Unless those damn cops took it. But why would they?

He moved the scarred maple rocker aside, looking behind it in the shadows. Mike was disappointed when it wasn't there.

"What are you seeking?" Pal asked from where he stood through the open door.

Mike swept aside the stacks of old newspapers with his arms. Some were over twenty-five years old. No one read a real newspaper any more.

News was sanitized and censored by the government, so it had to be received via the link. Real reading was suppressed. 'For public safety,' they said.

When, in fact, both he and Todd Road, and his loyal listeners, knew with absolute certainty that the government was out to control them as if they were cattle.

"My gun."

Pal moved to the ancient stone fireplace with its pile of black and gray ash in the hearth and the blackened stone running from the floor to the ceiling.

"You mean this?" Pal pulled the antique shotgun the cops didn't bother taking that hung off a rack that over the fireplace. They thought it too old to be much good. "I've studied your culture. I believe this is called a Remington." Pal hefted the shotgun, opened the barrel and slung it over his left arm like a veteran hunter.

Mike nodded, his eyes focused on the wooden slats of the floor. The floorboards creaked loudly as they moved across them.

"Yup. That it is, my good friend. Only that's not the one I'm looking for."

"Oh." Pal threw the rusted shotgun hard into the corner near a pile of rotting firewood where it clattered. The barrel snapped off its hinges and then sat in the corner like a twisted pile of black and orange pipe cleaners. He stood and faced Mike. "I can use my ships scanners to find it."

Mike, unfazed by the alien's sudden offer of assistance, let a slow grin cross his features. "You can do that?"

"Provided you tell me its composition, dimensions, and approximate weight, yes."

Mike hurried into the small, trash-filled kitchen at the rear of the house. There was a round, wooden table lying on its side, a porcelain sink with a dirty ring around it filled with rancid water, and a mold-covered tile counter-top with the drawers all open.

Mike pulled a piece of soil-covered paper and a blue ball-point pen from one of the drawers. He leaned against the counter after he wiped away some of the mold away with his shirt sleeve.

His pink tongue stuck out one side of his mouth as he began to draw a picture of the item he was searching for.

After several minutes of concentrated effort he showed what he'd drawn to Pal. "This. Can you find this?"

Pal squinted in the dim light and studied the crude drawing. He nodded. "Yes. It should be no problem. Does it have an internal energy source?"

"Yup, but it's probably dead."

Pal walked outside and the ramp, which had retracted when they went inside the log building, extended to greet him. He walked up it, leaving a trail of muddy footprints behind him. As he neared the top of the ramp, Mike gaped in amazement at the muddy footprints that faded, then disappeared completely.

"Some maid service," he muttered.

The ramp again disappeared into the ship, along with the doorway, until the ship was again a smooth unblemished surface. How do they do that?

Mike shook his head, turned, and headed back inside. It felt good to be home.

He sighed as he surveyed the wreckage of the log house. The cops had broken everything he cared about.

Family heirlooms were smashed to splinters and scattered about as if some mad cow had rampaged through the four-room dwelling.

He moved to a pile of broken dishes in the kitchen. They weren't expensive, but that wasn't the point. They were his. He knelt and picked up a jagged remnant of a plain white china plate and studied it. Pity.

He felt a sudden surge of anger from deep in his belly, then quickly quelled the feeling. An icy cold crept through him. The bastards were going to pay.

Mike was startled when Pal abruptly appeared in the doorway. In the alien's right hand he held a portable lamp with a metal handle.

The light from the lamp was incredibly bright; so much so he was unable to look directly at it without having to shield his eyes.

"I thought a light might be useful," said Pal. His red eyes were free of any expression and his pale face impassive.

Mike nodded. "You find my — item?"

"Yes, sir. It is approximately three meters below where you are standing."

The basement. The workshop. Yeah, with his tools.

It had to be. That made sense.

"Okay, follow me," said Mike.

Mike walked across the room to the pile of broken, cracked, and shredded furniture lying in one corner of the room. With Pal's help they managed to remove the bits and pieces of wood and cloth to reveal a trap door. This would let them into the basement.

There was a metal strap which originally had been held in place by a key lock. The lock was no longer there, and the steel strap that held down the door was bent out of shape, having been forced with something.

The throw rug that had once covered the access to the basement was nowhere to be seen. He concluded the cops must have removed it as evidence. He smirked.

Lot of good it did them.

He pulled hard on the brass handle laying flat in a recessed slot in the door, then heaved the heavy door upward.

It creaked loudly in the quiet, covering them in a shower of dust that had collected since he'd last been here.

He coughed and tried to wave the cloud away with his free hand. Pal just stood silently and watched him. The dust didn't seem to bother him. He glanced back and grinned at the alien.

"Follow me," he said as he headed down the stairs into the darkness below.

Pal followed immediately behind him, holding the portable lamp aloft in one pale hand. The light from the lamp adjusted for any decrease in darkness, becoming brighter the further down the creaking wooden stairs into the basement they went.

Once at the bottom they were struck by an earthy smell. The dirt walls were held back by flat lengths of treated wood supported by two-by-six stakes driven into the dirt floor. The boards had a greenish tinge, however the cabin was older than the wood. The planks were cracked in several places from the weight of the earth pressing against it. It wouldn't be long before the walls collapsed and buried the basement beneath a landslide of rock and earth.

Near one wall was a piece of plastic-coated wire, likely from an ancient clothes line. It was strung across the room, tied at each end to two-by-four boards. The compression caused by the dirt pressing against the boards had caused the line to sag in the middle. The metal clips were still attached where Mike had hung news clippings of his victims.

Mike gazed at the empty clips. At the time of his trial he'd lamented that he'd been unable to keep those clippings. The bastards thought he didn't deserve to have his property. He shook his head at the memory.

From the corner of one eye, he caught Pal studying his expression with interest.

The alien reminded him of the dog he'd had as a kid — it had watched him with the same studied expression when he'd been burning crickets alive in the backyard. That dog was still buried in the yard. Only he knew the exact spot of Barney's grave.

"Nothing," he said softly, his voice cracking with emotion. He'd loved his dog. "Move closer."

Pal moved to stand beside him in the center of the room. The lamp now lit every corner.

The roughed-in room contained piles of soiled, ripped cloth and rusting chains. Deep, dark red stains were mixed in with the gray soil. The ground was covered in footprints made by the boots of the cops and forensic investigators, markers of their intrusion into his private domain.

The deep-treaded depressions left by their boots reminded him of the footprints left on the moon by the astronauts, to mark their few landings on that barren, airless world.

Anger boiled inside him as he surveyed the haphazard pattern of the prints and the careless way they'd trashed the room.

Had these people no shame? He shook his head in disgust.

"Is something wrong?" asked Pal, staring at him with a puzzled expression on his pale face.

"Nope." With a vicious grin pasted to his pale features, Mike crossed to the room to the corner where there was a shredded pile of old clothes nearly rotted away to nothing.

The alien pointed to one corner of the room. He said, "A little over a meter."

The metallic smell mixed with the earth was strong in this corner of the room. Mike knelt down, shoved the pile of rags aside, then with his bare hands began to dig where the pile had been.

The earth was still soft. He managed to dig eighteen inches into the ground when he hit something metallic. Good. It hadn't been disturbed.

That meant the cops hadn't found it. They must have used DNA scanners and found the bodies buried toward the center of the room. DNA scanners wouldn't have helped them find this tool of his trade.

He grinned at Pal who now stood over him, watching intently as Mike uncovered a dented, green metal box with a steel latch down the front. Much of the paint was peeled away to reveal the bare steel beneath, which was slowly turning the color of brown rust.

There was an open padlock hooked through the steel loop of the latch that had once been secured. Mike pulled it out of the hole and laid it flat on the floor at his knees. He flipped the latch aside, then opened the box to reveal that, indeed, what he'd been seeking had been found. He grinned.

"What is it?" said Pal, his head cocked like a curious puppy. His red eyes narrowed as he studied the strange object. Mike gently pulled it out of the box as if it were the Holy Grail, cradling it in both hands; it was the one he'd

"I call her, 'ol Betsy." He hefted the electro shock gun he'd fashioned himself all those years ago. He'd used it to stun all of his victims, from his first to his last, before he'd buried it when the cops closed in on the farm. The electro shock gun helped him kill slowly. Guns were too messy and too quick. He enjoyed watching his victims suffer.

The device's all-plastic construction had made it undetectable in a world that used metal scanners and similar devices to detect technology that might be a threat. Betsy was old-school, an anachronism in this high-tech age. Sure the power source was depleted long ago, but that was no problem. He'd get another.

He spent the first year in captivity cursing himself for being so careless and letting himself get caught. This time, however, he wasn't going to make the same mistake. He'd taken care of Holly, now he had other scores to settle. First among them was the woman responsible for putting him on death row. The one stupid broad that got away and led them right to him.

He recalled the look in Agent Cody's eyes when she burst through the cabin door with her VLE pointed at him. She'd wanted to kill him where he stood. She would come to regret not pulling the trigger that day.

He smiled at Pal and placed the five-inch long electro shock gun into the pocket of his prison coverall.

"We gotta go shoppin', then we got some huntin' to do."

Pal nodded his head in agreement ,with a silly, happy grin on his face as if he were a child. For advanced beings, they clearly didn't understand murder; but he'd teach them, or he'd die trying. Mike wanted to laugh at his own joke, but stopped himself. He must act dignified.

TWELVE

TODD WALKED OUT the front door of the Ronald Regan Memorial Hospital and took a deep breath that caused him to wince due to sore ribs on his left side.

His favorite gray slacks were wrinkled from the courier bag that his maid service had used to ship them to him in, but what the hell, wrinkled pants were better than a few extra wrinkles in him.

He scanned the busy street with the air cars drifting slowly by him in the bottleneck of the morning's rush hour. They may not be burning fossil fuels, and they were not allowed above three feet from the ground, but they were the most efficient and safest people-movers in human history. Unfortunately, it hadn't always been that way.

Early experiments with skyways had ended in disaster a few years back with horrendous crashes and loss of life. Now only cops and other emergency services were permitted to fly high above the streets.

He'd railed against their construction at the time, but no one listened to a right-wing talk show host's opinion until it was too late. He'd gotten pretty good ratings when it came out he'd been against the skyway project.

'Another government boondoggle' he'd called it at the time. Well now they better get damned used to him being right.

He'd be an honest to goodness American hero after he helped the FBI re-capture Mike, and saved the human race from the aliens.

Gazing to his left, he saw a group of people dressed in suits standing near the street. Some held vid transcribers while others held e-pads.

Reporters.

When they saw Todd they hurried in his direction, running like bloodhounds that'd caught the scent of their prey. There had to be twenty or twenty-five of them. Todd straightened his shoulders and cleared his throat, then trotted out his best Hollywood smile. The spotlight was his. With the station manager dead and only himself and poor Amy left to run things, they'd be calling the shots at KZAP from now on.

The reporters began to hurl questions at him, the resonance of their voices like a wall of staccato-like fire from a battery of machine guns as they approached. Some even elbowed the others to get closer to him. He stood and watched their frantic competition with glee, his hands stuffed in his pockets. He'd gotten their attention — the story about Mike and the aliens had legs.

"Mr. Road, how do you feel about Mike Sikes's escape…?"

"What about your boss's death…?"

"How's Ms. Rickland...?"

Todd listened for several seconds, studying them like an anteater gazing at his dinner. "Ladies and gentlemen of the press —"

He was cut off by a sudden burst of a siren. He cowered covering his head with his hands as he felt the rush of air being displaced above him, his pant-legs flapping about as if hit by a strong wind. Todd stole a glance upward and saw flashing red and blue lights on the roof of a steel gray police air car about to land near him.

The reporters that had been converging on him scattered, reminding him of a startled herd of wildebeest on the African plains that he'd seen in old vids .

The African plains were empty now, ravaged by disease and poachers. But the wild confusion of the reporters as they ran in every direction to get away from the descending air car certainly looked like uncontrolled and startled animals.

He stepped back as the air car settled on its tripod landing gear and the passenger door flipped upward to reveal a scowling Angela Cody.

She wore a burgundy suit with a matching shirt underneath. Her matching low-slung leather sandals hit the pavement as soon as the door was up enough.

Once clear of the door she moved toward him, her hard gaze boring into him like a diamond drill.

Todd recalled part of an old expression. Something about 'looks killing the golden goose.' He was sure that if Agent Cody had her way, his goose would be cooked for sure.

"Huh—nice suit, Agent Cody," said Todd.

"Cut the small talk, Road. You're coming with me."

She gripped his left arm tightly and practically dragged him to the rear passenger door of the police air car. Her driver, a uniformed local cop, had already cycled the door open.

Angela shoved Todd in. He thought about saying something, and opened his mouth to speak.

She glared fiercely at him, which made him snap his mouth closed without saying anything. Now was obviously not the time to make small talk, or any other kind of talk. Her partner was dead and she didn't appear in the mood.

She sat in the front seat and after both doors were secured, they lifted off, leaving the crowd of angry reporters behind.

The reporters waved their fists angrily at Todd and Agent Cody, their faces distorted by rage. Some of the reporters recorded the air car lifting off with their vid cameras.

Todd turned his attention to Angela who held a portable data pad in her left hand and was tapping the keys with a red-tipped fingernail of her other hand. She was intent on her task, so Todd eased back into the comfortable seat.

He let out a soft sigh and let his body relax. The tension of the past few days had been excruciating on his system.

He watched the glass and steel towers of the city skyline passing beneath them. He wondered where they were going, when a dark building loomed ahead sticking through the overcast sky. It was considerably taller than the others that surrounded it; they would have to go much higher to clear it.

He'd never been in the building before. He didn't much care for government agencies that worked behind closed doors in their ivory — or in this case, darkly shaded, towers.

On the roof of the building was a landing pad, surrounded by a row of dazzling orange lights to mark it. The pilot set the car right in the middle of the circular platform with a slight bump, and the whine of the engine slowed. The doors in front of them gradually cycled open. Todd stepped out, then smoothed his navy blazer with his moist palms. Angela was making him uncomfortable with her glares and serious manner. Did the woman ever lighten up?

"Come on, Road."

Not waiting for him, Angela headed away from the landing pad as soon as her door opened, toward an elevator that would take them deep into the bowels of the building.

Todd hesitated when he saw the pilot still in his seat. The man's eyes were focused straight ahead. The car powered up lifted off and disappeared over the edge of the roofline.

Angela must have read his mind.

"He'll wait in the garage," she said without turning to look back at him.

Todd hurried after her. They got into the elevator and she said her floor number. The elevator scanned them, a security system designed to prevent intruders' entering the building, then began to move. Since the alarm didn't activate, Todd assumed his DNA had already been added to the device's database.

Todd didn't feel any sensation of movement, yet they were carried quickly to their destination and, in what seemed like seconds, were walking down the hall to Angela's office cubicle.

Once there she sat at her desk and plugged her data pad into a receptacle built in her desk designed to accept the interface. The data would be downloaded to her master server file in the blink of an eye.

Todd took a seat across from her when she sat back in her fabric covered executive chair. Her hands were folded in her lap. Her expression was blank as she stared at him for several seconds without saying a word.

His armpits became damp as he fidgeted in his seat. Todd wondered why she brought him here. Angela didn't seem like the kind of woman who did anything without a good reason.

"What kind of man are you, Road?" she said, finally breaking her silence.

"What do you mean?"

"What do you think I mean?" There was something in the way she said it that unnerved him.

"Huh — I don't know?"

"To me you're the stupid son of bitch who helped a ruthless serial killer escape. And you're the one person who the aliens said they needed to let the bastard loose on the rest of us. I'd say you're the stupidest man on the planet." Her eyes spit fire at him.

"That's not fair I… "

"A lot of people died yesterday because of you, Road. Including some who were my friends." He saw a flicker of sadness cross her eyes then quickly disappear.

"I know," he said. "It's not my fault."

"I know," she said.

"What can I do to help?" Todd said not disgusting the anger in his voice.

Angela leaned forward to rest her arms on her desk and looked into his eyes. "You and I need to talk to the one who person made all this happen."

Todd looked at her perplexed until... It dawned on him who she was talking about.

Pie, the alien in the mother ship. He, or it, had sent his symbiot to do his dirty work. The Pel'Tak had to be the ones orchestrating these events.

One thing that puzzled him was how they'd managed to get Sikes past all the security guards at the Onyx building. When they'd arrived at the studio, the place was like an armed camp readying to go to war.

"How did Mike and Pal get past all the guards at the studio? I know they left in the alien shuttle. The news reports at least said that much."

Angela's expression changed to a sly grin. "We have vid."

"How? Who?" Now they were getting somewhere.

With the worldwide security net down, Todd thought they wouldn't have any record of the escape. Obviously the newsies hadn't managed to get hold of all the facts.

"Do you tell me you're sources?" she said.

"Actually under the new U.S. Constitution of 2027… "

Her smile disappeared to become serious again. "Come on, let's go to the media center. I'll show you what we have."

She stood and headed for the door. Todd rose and followed her.

The entered the media room where they were again alone. In fact, he hadn't seen anyone else in the building so far. Lots of work cubicles and offices, but no people. Very strange. He was suddenly overcome by a feeling of impending dread.

"Are they dead?" He blurted.

Cody looked at him, her eyes hard as obsidian. She didn't answer his question but he knew the answer. The results of the explosion must have been far worse than the press had told the public.

They entered the media room, and Road sat in one of the swiveled chairs surrounding large glossy boardroom table that was at least twenty feet long. The farthest wall was a giant vid screen.

"Cody. File six alpha," she said.

An image appeared of the roof of the Onyx Corporation tower. The haze of brown smog distorted the image slightly, but the vid camera must have been an expensive one, because it filtered out most of the distortion.

The image was centered on the alien shuttle, resting on struts extending from the smooth hull, sitting on the black and gray painted roof. Someone had moved it from the park to the roof of the building. This was the first time Todd had really had an opportunity to study the ship in any detail.

The alien craft's surface shimmered as if it was distorted, but everything else in frame was solid. This meant there was probably some kind of energy field surrounding it.

But what puzzled him more than anything was the absence of the police security force and the snipers.

"Where are the snipers?" he asked.

Angela smiled grimly and pointed at the monitor indicating he should continue to watch.

The image zoomed in to reveal two figures exiting the rooftop elevator and hurrying toward the shuttle. One was in prison coveralls, the other was definitely Pal.

They quickly boarded the shuttle and it immediately lifted off, rotated in a hover position 180 degrees, then with a blur of movement, disappeared into the sky and was gone. It happened so fast, the auto-tracker in the camera was unable to follow.

The image went off, leaving the flat black surface of the screen staring back at them.

"So we know how they escaped. But what does it mean?" he said.

"Did you see the time indicator at the bottom right of the screen?" said Angela.

"Huh, no."

"Cody, file alpha six. Freeze image at beginning of the segment."

The monitor did as instructed. The alien ship sat in the center of the screen again only it was frozen. Todd eyes shifted to the time indicator. His face paled.

"I don't know how they're doing it but I think the aliens are able track your movements from their ship in orbit. In fact I think they're watching us right now. Right here. They know where you are and what you're doing."

Cody's brow wrinkled. "How do you know?"

"The missing guards, the show, the explosion, they knew everything as it happened. They had to be watching, listening, our behavior is too unpredictable not to have an advantage to stay one step ahead of us. To know what we know." Todd turned to face Cody. "Think about it, our best spy satellites can eavesdrop on conversations, take close up digital images of actual events, but we can't read minds. Imagine the possibilities, the advantage, if we could."

Todd's mind whirled. He'd told Pie not to talk to him inside his head and so far the alien seemed to have granted him his privacy. He didn't specifically tell him not to listen. Pie was listening to his thoughts yet he was unaware of him. It was like Pie had a super spy satellite capable of reading thoughts over great distances.

Fuck!

This was impossible. He felt as if he were being raped.

"Cody alpha six. Take us back two minutes before the video starts."

There was more. The image shifted, and heavily-armed security teams and snipers peopled the rooftop. They stood in small groups talking. They obviously didn't expect anything to happen, this high up on the building.

Suddenly they all seemed to react to something they saw above them. They removed their VLE weapons from their shoulders and pointed the barrels skyward.

A sudden burst of light made Todd wince and look away. When the spots in front his eyes cleared he saw the cops were gone. They'd vanished as if they never existed.

"Same thing that happened to the limo?" said Todd.

"Nope. There was no explosion. We don't know what happened to them. By the time your show started, every security force member was suddenly gone."

"Well, you're still here."

"Yup, and my partner's definitely dead. At least that's what we told his widow."

"What do you want me to do?"

"Mr. Road, I want you to speak with those aliens inside your head. You told me they are able to talk with you telepathically. I want you talk with this 'Pie,' as you call him, and find out where Mike Sikes is so I can shoot the son of a bitch.

"I wish now I hadn't hesitated three years ago when I had the chance to send this guy to hell. I'm going to fix that mistake. Permanently. But we need a lot more information to find him. This is where you come in."

She was right. He had to help her. He didn't know how — or even if — the aliens would tell him where Mike was, but he had to try.

He had some responsibility for this mess. Sikes was on the loose. How horrible was that to even think about? He must be stopped.

"When do I start?" he said.

"Now's as good a time as any. How do you do it?"

A confused look came over Todd's face. "Do what?"

Angela pointed with one finger toward the white ceiling tiles that made up the roof of the boardroom. "How do you talk to them?"

"Um, I don't know, exactly. I just think inside my head. They read my thoughts and talk to me."

"Are they talking to you right now?"

"No."

"Okay, so how do you get them to talk to you?" Her lips were pressed into a thin red line.

Clearly she was losing patience with his responses.

Todd appeared contemplative for a second or two, then he said, "I told Pie to get out of my head when I was on the alien ship. He hasn't spoken to me since. I've no idea—"

"Tell him it's okay to talk inside your head again." Todd looked doubtful. "If you tell him it's okay, he might make contact again. Maybe you pissed him off like your pissing me off right now."

Todd shrugged and closed his eyes.

Pie, can you hear me?

Nothing but silence. His heart beat rapidly and he detected the slight odor of chocolate coming from the other side of the table. Cody must be a chocoholic.

Nothing. He concentrated harder. Pie, it's okay to talk inside my head again. I want you to, please. He winced. I sound whiny, even to me. God, I hate that.

Hello, Mr. Road. Todd almost jumped for joy.

It was Pie's voice, inside his head.

Maybe he'd always been there hovering near the edge of his consciousness like some brain-draining vulture.

Todd's eyes popped open and he looked wide-eyed at Angela, who was staring intently at his face. She smiled thinly as she saw him reacting to what he was hearing.

She eased back into her cushioned chair. She made a circular motion with one finger to indicate he should continue.

He nodded. "Huh, Pie where have you been?"

You sound a little stressed. Are you alright, Mr. Road?

"Sure I'm fine. " Todd felt like he was giving the weather report.

It was like he'd turned the clock back thirty years when he was fresh out of college and a cub reporter for KSNT in Boise. He shrugged his shoulders at Angela and mouthed asking for instructions.

"Ask him if he knows where Mike and his buddy are." Angela Cody's eyes sparkled. She was enjoying his discomfort.

He squirmed in his seat, the smell of salty perspiration, emitted by his own body invaded his nostrils.

"Huh, Pie, do you know where Mike is right now? And Pal?"

Yes.

"He said he does," Todd said to Angela. She bolted forward in her chair, giving him a start; her eyes filled with fire.

"Where?" She asked loudly, her anxious voice echoing off the walls of the boardroom.

"Pie, please tell me exactly where they are."

They are six point two miles from your location. Pie's voice was very calm. Too calm.

His eyes went wide and he hands began to tremble. "Oh, my God," he whispered.

"What? Where is he?" said Angela, reaching instinctively to the holster on her belt that held her automatic pistol.

"Close," whispered Todd. His eyes scanned the room as if he expected Mike Sikes to suddenly appear from thin air.

"Be a little more specific," said Angela standing up. She placed both hands flat on the table's slick, shiny surface and leaned forward to glare at him. "I want him. I want him now."

"He's in the city. Pie says within six hundred miles of here," said Todd, his voice trembled with fear. His stomach twisted into a knot. Maybe Mike was after him. He didn't want to die. He gazed at Angela whose brow was wrinkled in thought.

Her expression changed to one of frustration. "Oh, fuck," she said. "I don't know where he's going, but you and I are going to need some additional firepower when we do find him. I'm actually more worried about..."

She reached into a holder on her other hip and retrieved her personal link. She dialed a number, but, from her puzzled expression, there was obviously no answer.

Road pulled out his own link. No signal. The link must be dead. Of course this was impossible. It was as if the link network had suddenly ceased to exist.

The link had so many redundant back up systems it would never go down. Ever. In the past fifty years, the link net had never failed. Not once.

There could only be one possible reason. Somehow Pie and his friends had taken out the city's communication system — and maybe the world's — just as they'd taken out the surveillance net. But why would they?

Were they going to stand by and let Mike take another innocent life? If so, why?

Angela threw her link hard across the room where it shattered against the wall.

She glared at Todd, who cowered with his arms covering his bald head as he was showered with black and silver plastic and the chips from inside the link's outer casing.

"You and I are going to save lives, no matter what it takes. Got me?"

He peeked from beneath one arm and nodded sheepishly.

"You're a war veteran, aren't you, Road?"

Again, he nodded.

She hurried to the door and, after opening it, stood eyeing him impatiently. Todd sighed to himself, stood, moved to the door under her steady gaze,. then passed her into the hallway. Together they made their way down the bright corridor to a steel door recessed into the wall.

He could tell by the metal bolts sticking out where the hinges were. The metal strip that ran the outside circumference protected the door from being tampered with. Next to the door in the wall was a black number pad with raised white numbers in three rows, starting with zero ending with nine.

Angela keyed a sequence into the number pad so fast that her movements were a blur. Soon there was a soft beep as the door's locking mechanism disengaged.

A door handle appeared from a recessed slit in the door and she pulled it toward her, obvious strain in her arm, as it tightened to move the heavily armored door aside.

Once the door was open, he was hit with a musty scent that filtered out of the room. They entered an area of pure blackness until the overhead lighting system flickered and then came on, forcing him to momentarily shield his eyes.

When he could see, he stood there, his mouth hanging open. In the room were racks containing every conceivable type of weapon he'd ever seen, and a few he didn't recognize.

Angela began to pull weapons off the steel racks affixed to the walls. She selected two long, rifle-like weapons, one of which she tossed at him. It looked like a plastic water gun.

He caught it in both hands and realized it was heavier than it first appeared.

He hefted the gun, if that's what it was, and studied it. It had a large black chamber attached to the top of the steel-blue housing, much like the chamber on a kid's water gun designed to hold water. He shook it slightly, but didn't hear anything like that sounded remotely like water. In fact, he didn't hear much of anything at all, but he did feel the weight of the chamber shift as it moved.

The football-shaped holding tank had something heavy inside that shifted like a thick liquid. This was going to take some getting used to if he was expected to shoot anything with it.

"What is this thing?" said Todd.

Angela was busy pulling down a smaller, hand-held version of the same weapon. It looked like a water pistol.

"These weapons were developed by a top secret contractor. They do not exist on any government record. The money to pay for them — and believe me they are worth more than you make in a lifetime — comes from black ops funds.

"And if you ever talk to anyone about them, I'm going to have to kill you." She paused and raised one eyebrow. "I'm not kidding, Road. Don't test me.

"Grip the stock tight then switch it on using the gray button there," she pointed to the pistol grip at the three buttons, one gray, one white and one red. "You may feel a slight increase in temperature as it reads your DNA and locks its memory so no one else can use the weapon but you."

He chuckled nervously. "But I don't have clearance."

"I'm giving you clearance, Road." Her gaze said she was deadly serious.

He again studied the weapon. He guessed they were going to fight fire with fire. He did as instructed, and felt the hum of power in his hands as the weapon came alive and the warmth in the grip, just as she said, as it read his DNA. A green light on the barrel came on. The rifle was armed and ready.

"What do these different buttons do?"

"Need to know. And you don't need to know."

How about that, Pie?

I will not let you hurt him, Mr. Road, Pie responded in his head as if he were reciting a recipe for hot chocolate. "Ok, buddy."

Angela whirled to face him the rifle grasped at the ready, one nail polished finger poised over the trigger. Her other hand grasped the grip that ran along the barrel. Angela Cody reminded him of a marine.

Did he say that out loud?

"What did he say?" she demanded.

Yup, I guess I did. "He says they won't let us hurt him. I think they mean Sikes."

"Damn," she whispered.

This mess keeps getting weirder and weirder.

THIRTEEN

Angela led the way to the underground garage beneath FBI headquarters.

The aliens had created havoc, and, for some unknown purpose which she couldn't fathom, the politicians seemed to think they were so important that they were the next candidates for kidnapping by the aliens.

During the past hour the news channel labeled the aliens invaders rather than visitors.

Angela smirked and glanced over her right shoulder at a sweaty Todd Road.

She shook her head. She pitied him.

The guy could easily afford one of those 'personal trainers to the stars,' yet he still remained out of shape. Probably suffered from high blood-pressure, too.

Angela led the way across the quiet, shadowy parking garage, surrounded by the strong scent of oil and grease from the repair pool. Their footsteps echoed in the silence.

The heady odors wafted over them. Right now, though, her concentration was on the task at hand she had seemingly strengthened her constitution because she felt fully charged and ready for action.

She stopped beside an air car different than the one they'd used before. "Access code, Cody-one-six-Alpha-one-six-Cody."

"Security code recognized," said the car's voice interface. She instructed the security system to follow her verbal commands only. This, too, was acknowledged.

She couldn't chance Road getting panicked and taking off without her when things got rough. Angela was reasonably certain this case was going to get very bad indeed before it was over.

The car doors on both sides rose upward to allow them to enter the cockpit; they strapped themselves in, and Angela slipped the thin headset over her head. The GPS indicator on the dash blinked.

"The GPS works?" Todd said.

"Yeah. A few years ago our vehicles and a few essential satellites were hardened against EMP attack. The GPS sat was one of them."

Todd nodded, but he sensed somehow the aliens let them have the GPS satellite. Are they playing us? he wondered.

She smiled thinly at Road who attempted, but failed, to form a smile in return. His trembling hands gripped the barrel of the energy rifle, twisting around its hard, metallic surface as if he were attempting to tie the thing into a knot. His nervous eyes flitted about them as they lifted off and pulled out of the landing spot.

Angela ran a systems check as they cruised to the street access. Normally she would have done this prior to lift off, but time was short and Mike Sikes was going to be one slippery devil.

"I'll warn you now, Road. This is going to be a rough ride. The traffic control systems are down and there are a lot of panicked people out there. We'll stay above the maddened crowd as best we can, but its still going to be tough."

He nodded his round, pale, face a sheen of sweat.

Once above ground, she saw the situation was worse than she thought.

She carefully wove her way through the air cars speeding in every direction, heading ever upward. Her eyes scanned the screens in the dash in front of them searching for potential threats. Ten screens in a half moon shape around them gave them a 360 degree view of the sky surrounding the air car. Off to their right, a car grazed another and began to spin out of control toward the ground. Though heavily damaged, a trail of black smoke followed it across the brown haze of the sky. Both cars were on fire.

The other driver evidently was not as skilled a pilot as the other operator. There were no parachutes. Except for emergency vehicles air cars were normally only allowed three feet off the ground, maximum. Today though all bets were off. They were flying forty feet above the street like a panicked herd of cattle. Way above the survivable altitude if the driver was forced to jump.

Angela watched the man leap clear of his flaming vehicle and fall to his death. Panic did strange thing to ones psyche. The guy flapped his arms as if he were a featherless bird all the way to the life ending pavement far below.

The gathered crowd stood in rapt awe, gazing up at the aerial carnage, much like a crowd attending some ancient Roman gladiatorial contest. They scattered like wheat as the man hit the ground in a sudden burst of bloody red spray.

The damaged car hovered monetarily then followed its owner to the street where it exploded in a fireball to consume the man's shattered corpse.

The city was in chaos.

"Everything's gone to hell," he said.

Angela, focused on getting them out of the area as quickly as possible, steering them around another fiery collision.

Todd gripped the sides of his seat as he was alternately floated against the restraint then pressed hard into his seat as she made tight turns to guide them safely.

Finally they were clear of the city and headed toward open sky. Todd thought the blue clear sky never looked so welcoming.

They passed the river where high speed police patrol boats, their water jets screaming, bounced over the light chop of the murky water. Rooster tails of water followed them downriver, headed away from the city.

They left the river behind and flew over the ring of green forest that circled the city. This was the green belt meant to clear the air of pollutants. Throughout the stands of ancient oaks were gray sticks of dead firs and hemlock trees that the brown haze had claimed. The oaks were the stubborn ones of the lot, and refused to succumb.

Finally, after leaving the city behind ten miles out, Angela made it to a clear patch of sky and hovered over a small two lane dirt road.

"So many lives shattered by a monster," Angela said softly as she gazed out the window.

"I saw you press the white button on your pistol. Why?"

She shook her head. "Need to know."

FOURTEEN

Mike held the light as Pal pressed against the door at the rear of the little hardware store.

The farm was long behind them by the time they landed in darkness just outside Kelletville, a small town in rural Wisconsin. Mike knew this town well.

Little Cindy James had lived here. He remembered watching her for days as she came and went from the elementary school. She was nine when he first saw her, and twelve when he'd taken her.

She was one of many that the FBI had never been able to pin on him. Not that they hadn't tried.

The cops were sure stupid. They satisfied themselves with what they had from that one place. They hadn't looked beyond their noses and checked all the missing persons over the past two decades.

If they had they would have found beautiful little Cindy.

She was a sweet young thing. Pure, black hair in gentle curls, with skin the color of new snow, so soft to the touch. Her appearance reminded him of a little princess.

He recalled the piercing, pale sapphire eyes staring at him while he worked his magic. He recalled those same eyes staring lifeless at him before he filled in the pit where he'd buried her corpse.

Yup, she was a pretty thing. He even remembered exactly where she lay.

Maybe I'll dig her bones up one day. They'd make a nice souvenir.

His recollections were interrupted when Pal pressed his body weight against the door until it gave way with a resounding crack. Pal stopped the door from banging against the inside wall by grabbing the round faux-brass door handle.

Going first, with the light held in front of him, Mike stepped inside.

The strong odor of fertilizer hit him as he walked toward the front of the store.

He recalled the battery display rack. He hadn't been here in over twenty-five years, but the town seemed unchanged since the day he'd moved on.

The light's glow illuminated rows of garden tools, spades, rakes, and work gloves all neatly organized in shelves and labeled so the customers could find what they were looking for. He passed the garden hose display; green, yellow, and blue hoses all coiled and standing on their sides. Finally, he found the battery display rack.

There were batteries of every kind. The old fashioned D and C cells, to the more modern link battery packs designed to hold their charge for a year before they needed to be reenergized. At the bottom of the rack, in a cardboard box were the odd-sized batteries. It was among these Mike found what he was looking for.

He held the battery up to the light to study it. The black plastic housing with the dual plugs at one end were the perfect fit for the weapon. They would fit easily into the receptacles for his electro shock gun, and the battery's energy would allow him to kill at will.

The label said the battery would last five hours of continuous use before it needed to be recharged. No one would stop him now.

Mike smiled. "This is what we need." Pal nodded.

Suddenly there was a burst of light as a beam from a high-intensity flashlight swept the room. "Hey, what are you two doin'?" said a gruff man's voice.

It must be the shop owner Mike concluded. His mouth formed a twisted grin. He might be good practice for the gun; he hadn't used a weapon in a long time. A thrill surged up from his belly. He glanced at Pal. The alien looked as placid as before.

And so the teacher begins to teach.

From the left pocket of his coverall he pulled out the electro shock gun and slipped the battery into the receptacle. A perfect fit.

He hit the switch and there was a hum as power surged through. The electro shock gun warmed up and began to emit a low hum.

Mike scurried to hide among the shelves. He peeked around the corner of a shelf of plumbing parts.

A man wearing a blue-and-white striped floor length housecoat came toward Pal with a double-barreled shotgun leveled at Pal's chest. His steel-gray hair was in disarray and he wore wire-rimmed, steel glasses. Gray stubble covered his narrow face. His eyes narrowed as he studied the red-eyed alien.

"Don't I know you?" he said, his shotgun unwavering. He moved closer and adjusted his glasses with one hand, keeping the other on the gun.

He stopped and stared at Pal, his eyes suddenly wide. "Oh shit...."

Mike chose that moment to burst from behind the shelf and rush the old man. Before the man could react, Mike had the twin electrodes pressed into the center of the man's chest.

A wide grin crossed his face when he depressed the trigger.

A burst of lightning from the gun hit the old man square in the chest. His body trembled from the force of the electrical energy that traveled through him. He jerked, unable to control his body, and his eyes blinked from the pain. His hair shot up like a gray halo around his head, and the gun flew out of his hands to land on the floor with a clatter..

After several seconds, Mike let go of the trigger and the lightning stopped. The old man collapsed, falling forward to land face first with a loud smack. The smell of ozone, mixed with feces and urine, filled the room. Mike loved the smell of death.

His body was smoking as Mike moved toward him.

"Little too much juice," said Mike with a shrug of his narrow shoulders. "Kinda fun though, don't you think?"

Pal stood still, his red eyes emotion-free. Mike stood and faced the alien, eyeing him suspiciously. "Any of this bother you?"

"Not at all," said Pal, his tone flat.

"Good, because we got a lot more to take care of before I'm done."

Mike walked over to the display rack and retrieved two additional batteries from the cardboard box.

As they headed out the broken rear door Mike decided to fully educate Pal in the fine art of death.

They entered the shuttle, lifted off, and disappeared into the dark moonless night.

FIFTEEN

ANGELA GLANCED AT Todd with a small smile on her lips. "Nice ride?" she asked.

He nodded, but an angry frown marred his forehead. "We could've been killed."

Angela laughed brightly. "Com'on, Road. Think. Can you really blame these people? The world has suddenly erupted into chaos, and an insane killer is on the loose with the very aliens who brought down civilization as we know it."

Todd thought for a moment then said, "Yeah, I guess you're right." Todd gazed the passing fields far below them as they moved through the daytime sky.

"Where we goin'?" said Todd.

"Good question," replied Angela.

She punched a button and the screen set into the dashboard of the air car lit up. Todd gazed at the glowing screen and immediately recognized the document displayed, even though it was marked CONFIDENTIAL.

It was her investigation file.

Somehow she'd managed to download the complete file on the Sikes case before the link was compromised.

The file had been the subject of much speculation by the news media. The vid broadcast every night during Mike's show trial had focused on the closed FBI file sitting on the prosecution's table next to the Assistant District Attorney.

Todd cringed at the recollection of that mealy-mouthed man with his blue pinstriped suits, red power tie, and sparkling white teeth. Blake Hemple, the ADA who looked more like Hollywood than any actor ever could, was confident, smart, and 'a dedicated servant of the people,' as he coined the term.

Todd scanned the first page of the report.

He was finally getting the chance to read the report that had been eyes-only during the trial. But what he read in the first few paragraphs made him think he should have reconsidered. There was a twinge deep in the pit of his stomach and he swallowed the bile that hit the back of his throat with an acid taste.

"What are we looking for?"

Angela frowned. "I don't know exactly. So far Sikes has taken out his lawyer; of course, we're out of contact with headquarters, so he might've killed everyone in Ohio by now. If there's one thing the son of a bitch is good at, it's killing."

"Maybe he's after the woman that escaped," Todd suggested casually as his eyes fell on her name at the bottom of the first page.

He glanced up when he felt Angela grab his left arm. She gripped him so hard he wondered if she was ever going to let go.

She looked at him her eyes wide. "I think you're on to something, Road. Yeah, that makes sense. Sikes hates loose ends. That would fit his profile. That and revenge for her fingering him to the locals."

Much to Todd's relief, Angela let go of his arm and steered the car into a tight one-hundred and eighty degree turn. The car was at its top speed when she made the turn.

"Hey!" Todd yelped as he was shoved hard against the door by the centrifugal force. His seat belt strained to hold him. He gripped the door handle with both hands.

"Are we going back to the city?"

She glanced at him with her hard eyes and a wry grin on her narrow features. "Where do you think?" she said.

"Oh, shit..." he whispered. "I don't know if that's a good idea, Agent Cody. Later after things come down, sure, but now?"

She nodded. "Yeah, it's probably dangerous but we have to find the one that got away before Sikes does." Her eyes narrowed. "Or she dies, of that I'm certain."

***

Angela flew the car slowly through city streets deserted as the sky grew dark, the sun having disappeared below the horizon only ten minutes earlier. Using her dashboard map she easily located the street where Azelia Marks last lived.

So far they'd been stopped four times by heavily-armed National Guard patrols consisting of twin air cars mounted with laser cannons. The heavier models were designed for maximum kill zone coverage, and flanked by shock troopers with their auto mag VLE's at the ready.

The trooper's emotionless gaze studied them from beneath their Kevlar helmets with bullet proof face shields. Their dark green body armor was non-reflective so they were hard to see until they suddenly appeared before them like green ghosts in the evening gloom.

Each time, the senior officer in charge checked Angela's credentials and ran a weapon scan of the air car. After he finished he grunted and waved them on.

They would go a short distance further, and then be stopped again.

Angela was becoming agitated by the whole thing when they finally arrived at Azelia Marks' street.

Angela fixed her eyes on the ancient brownstone walkups lining both sides of the streets. Most were dark. Only a few of the townhouses had on lights.

Angela stopped when the green icon on the screen began to flash intermittently.

"We're here. Follow me." The car settled on the pavement. The driver's door swung open, and before Todd could say anything Angela had stepped out onto the dark, shadowy street.

Reluctantly, Todd joined her.

Angela pulled her jacket aside to reveal her service pistol. She rested one hand on the butt as she moved to the rear of the car. Todd moved to stand beside her, his heart race increasing. Todd looked at her wonderingly.

He gripped the stock of the energy rifle tighter. A trickle of perspiration ran down Todd's back.

Angela went to the trunk and pulled out another energy rifle. Reaching over to his weapon she flicked a switch on the side of Todd's rifle and the gun emitted a soft hum. She did the same with hers.

He felt the transfer of power from the weapon's stock through his hands then into his body. Angela showed him the release mechanism on the stock of the energy gun. Testing it, he slid the heavy plastic slider switch which caused a section of the barrel to open, revealing a scope which extended upward from a compartment built into the barrel. Then a crimson laser-like beam of light appeared from the barrel end of the gun. The barrel narrowed to a tip, not for projectile weapons but to focus the energy to a single point thereby concentrating the beam.

She grinned at him. "Almost as good as sex it's it?"

Grinning sheepishly, he slid the switch to the off position and the laser light disappeared and the scope retracted.

Quickly repeating the procedure with her own weapon, Angela led him at a near-run toward the three-story brownstone that was their destination.

The iron railing running along the stairs was rusted and scored as if by a sharp object. The stone stairs themselves weren't much better. They were chipped and cracked from age and abuse.

Angela went up two stairs at a time, then stood at the top waiting for Todd to catch up. He reached the top step, puffing under the weight of the energy gun; Angela's breathing was as level and as even as it was at the bottom of the steep steps.

Once at the top the targeting beams from the guns cast a reddish glow over the brick. Angela held her rifle against her hip. Still gasping, Todd stood behind her, studying the front door. The locks on these old buildings were pretty flimsy by modern standards, so they should easily gain entry, besides the door was comprised of a wood frame surrounding glass.

Angela told him stand to the right side of the door, she was going to lead them inside. He nodded, scanning the area around them for visible threats as he moved out of the way.

Angela took a step backward then directed a kick with her low-heeled leather shoes directly on the brass lock. There was a crack as the doorframe gave way and the door flew in, banging loudly against the wall shattering the glass. Coops...

Holding his breath, Todd strained to hear any reaction from within the apartment or from the street outside. The only sounds that greeted them was the sound of a dog barking far off in the distance, and his own heart as it beat rapidly in his ears.

Exhaling slowly to calm his nerves, he followed Angela as she made her way inside. They alternated going ahead deeper into the dark building, with one of them hanging back to keep watch over their probing partner.

Finally, it was too nearly dark to immediately see any potential threat. After several seconds their eyes adjusted and they began to edge slowly forward again, up a flight of sagging wooden stairs visible in the gloom. Angela went more slowly this time, taking one step at a time so Todd could keep up with her.

They moved to the upper floor where there was a second glass door that led to a corridor. Todd noted the torn and parched wallpaper, with a faded red rose pattern, that adorned the hallway as they made their way down the empty, silent hall. The rust-colored carpet beneath them was worn through to the plywood floor beneath. Their footsteps echoed off the tight walls.

Their breathing was ragged as they moved, the heavy weapon held at the ready. Finally, Angela held one hand up in a fist to indicate they'd arrived. She signaled him to stand to one side of the darkly-stained wooden door. There on the chipped and scarred door, in stylized black plastic numbers, was the number 217.

They paused and Todd strained to hear anything coming from the other side of this door. Silence. Stale cooking smells invaded his senses. His nose wrinkled. Yuck, cabbage.

This search took him back to his days in the Special Forces when his team was dispatched to capture a key terrorist cell leader in Beirut, early in the third Gulf War. During that operation they'd moved from building to building until they'd cornered the man in an apartment.

Eerily like this one actually. His sense of déjà vu was screaming at him to be cautious as it had back then.

Unfortunately that episode ended badly. He hoped this one would be more successful

He pushed the thoughts away and refocused on the task at hand.

Angela signaled she was going first. With the beam of light from her rifle centered on the worn brass doorknob, her weapon discharged striking the door. The area around the door knob and the knob itself glowed brightly then disintegrated in microseconds.

Angela kicked the door in with one fluid motion. Todd rushed in after her. The apartment reeked of ozone and stale urine. Todd wrinkled his nose, which was under assault by the putrid smells.

Together they swept the dark room using only the light from their weapons. The living room contained a worn, sagging brown sofa, an old-style vid sitting against one wall, and a cheap, pressboard end table, with a tawdry, canary-yellow lamp sitting on it. The forest green wallpaper on the walls was ripped in places, stained white plaster showing through beneath. The room was musty and didn't have the look or feel of being occupied recently. It looked deserted.

Angela rushed toward the only door that led off the main room. As she reached it she dropped a shoulder and burst through the door ,keeping her body low to avoid being a good target. That room too was empty.

Todd moved to a hallway he spotted that led off the main room, crouching low as he moved down the empty hallway until he came to the kitchen. He swept the stained and worn tiles that made up the floor with his light, and saw a small splotch of red near the twin steel sinks set into one wall.

Sitting on the cracked counter top beside the sink was a half-finished bottle of whiskey. The cap was missing and the amber liquid gleamed as the light played over it.

A small window over the sink was open and the sheer white curtains that hung on either side, billowed as a light breeze rolled through the open window, carrying with it the scent of rotten garbage from the alley below. Todd ignored the smell as he moved to the sink and focused the spotlight on the red splotch on the counter. It could be dried blood.

Angela came up beside him and gazed at the spot of red. She removed her hand-held DNA scanner from her suit jacket and ran it over the spot.

In the dim light from their combined spotlights, Todd saw her frown. She pulled back one of the stained curtains and looked out the window, then back at her scanner's readout.

When she didn't say anything he asked, "What is it?"

"The DNA readout reads we missed her by an hour," she said, her voice low and tight. "He's got her."

"It can do that?" She nodded.

Though it was a warm evening a sudden chill shot through him,.

"Fuck," he said under his breath. "Do you think she's dead?"

She shook her head, her eyes misted over when she gazed into his. "I don't know, but not if we find her in time."

His veins ran with ice water; this was his fault. He'd made a circus of Mike Sikes to get a greater market share. Due to his corporate-driven mentality, more innocents would pay with their lives.

The bastard must be stopped. Todd gripped the barrel of the energy weapon tighter and he felt anger begin to burn in the pit of his stomach.

"Come on, Road, we've got work to do."

She walked out of Azelia Marks' kitchen, leaving him alone. He stared at the open, half-empty bottle of whiskey sitting on the cracked, dirt-covered counter.

He turned and left the room. He thought about asking Angela about the red button but realized he didn't really want or need to know. The weapon was a VLE smart gun, like her service pistol, so he instinctively knew anyway.

Red to kill, and white to wound and capture. Todd recalled the outrage when Mike was caught alive. This time white was definitely not an option.

***

After Todd and Angela were airborne again, they headed east headed for Quantico, Virginia. There were many places where Sikes used to hide his victims while he tortured them, so they needed a lot more information. FBI headquarters contained a powerful database of profile data, code named GIANT, gathered from the hundred years. The data would aid them in their search.

It was going to be like looking for that certain penny in a wishing well.

It sickened Todd to think of all the places where the monster had hidden his victims around the country before he'd been caught.

Until Mike was discovered, serial killings were ancient history. Mental illness was a thing of the past.

Today, technology took care of what people used to call psychopaths. The combination of new drugs therapies, and micro-brain surgery had been perfected in the past twenty years.

It meant the so-called 'mentally ill' were now productive members of modern society. In all of human history, the human race never experienced such a medical renaissance. Too bad this treatment failed with Sikes. No one had been able to explain why, just that the medical treatments didn't work.

Mike Sikes was an anomaly, a dinosaur, a throwback to the dark times. The death penalty had been specially resurrected just for him.

A special act of Congress declared all previous laws against the death penalty to be set aside in this exceptional case.

Massive public support for the execution of Mike Sikes had led to Congress changing the law passing a bill allowing them to enact any law they saw fit to provide a safe and secure America. Fear trumped freedom.

The press dubbed the law the "Mike Sikes Act." Mike Sikes must die if people were to feel safe once again. He would be the last execution in the history of the world.

They reached the FBI building without being detained by any further National Guard patrols, much to Todd's relief. He sensed Angela wasn't about to be so cooperative, given her mood after the most recent failure.

They rode the elevator to her office where they again went into the boardroom and sat side by side in two chairs at one end of the long board table.

After uttering her verbal authorization, she commanded GIANT to bring up and display the Sikes case file.

"GIANT, begin playback, one page at a time. Stop at any reference to a location be it town, city, or shack, known to be frequented by Sikes in the past," said Angela.

After the two seconds it took GIANT to download the complete report — all five hundred and sixteen volumes of it — it began to playback the official record as instructed. After another three minutes the playback stopped on page three of volume one with the place name highlighted in red.

Todd squinted at the monitor on the desk in front of him then at the large vid screen. "New Denver," Todd murmured.

"Nope," said Angela. Bitterness edged her tone. She threw the black ballpoint she'd been fidgeting with across the table in disgust.

"This is going to take forever," said Todd gazing at the document on the screen. "How do we know which one is the one we're looking for?"

"We don't," said Angela bluntly. "I'll know. Good, old-fashioned cop stuff, Road. Instinct. That's how I caught him the last time, and that's how I'll catch him again."

Todd studied the determined expression on her face and thought for a fleeting second he should challenge her. She'd needed the Marks girl to escape to break the case.

Unless Azelia Marks was very lucky this time and managed to escape from Mike's grasp again, Angela wouldn't have such a break this time.

And there was the wild card thrown in of the aliens. How would they react if she got close to nailing the bastard, and what would they do if Angela killed Sikes?

These were questions for which he didn't necessarily want the answers.

Without a link, or any other means of obtaining a viable lead they were pretty much in the dark, and if he was reading her right Angela Cody was feeling the same frustration he was.

"You can call me, Todd y'know." His eyebrows arched as he said it.

She glanced away from the large wall-vid monitor, her green eyes sparkling as she smirked. "Yeah, sure — Road."

SIXTEEN

BUDDY, MICHIGAN; Harm, Vermont; Buick, Delaware… small towns across the country. Names of places Todd had never heard of. But these places were some of the towns across the country where Mike kept his lairs, and the torture chambers where he murdered his victims.

Todd studied the glowing white screen with its black lettering containing the names as the computer highlighted each one in the report. The image on the vid monitor was a three-dimensional representation of all fifty five states of the United States, from the southernmost border to the arctic, across the territory formerly known as Canada.

As each city was discounted by Angela — and he could detect no reason why she would discount some immediately, and study the related information on others closely, before she grumbled then discounted those as well — a red dot on the map would change to black. There were still far more red dots on the map than black ones.

Todd sighed heavily, which caused Angela to glance up at him.

Her normally intense gaze was dulled by the hours they'd been at this, and the dark circles under her eyes were evidence of the fatigue beginning to settle in on both of them.

"Tired, Road?" she said dully. Her words slurred slightly as she spoke.

He nodded then pinched the bridge of his nose with his fingers. His eyeballs made a clicking as he blinked, which meant his eyes were dry and he was nearing end of his ability to stay awake. He nodded in silence.

"Yeah, me too," she said. "Let's take a break."

She shoved her chair back and plucked her rumpled suit jacket off the back.

"Computer. Hold search." The image on the map froze, as did the e-pages that appeared on the monitors embedded in the boardroom table.

Todd's mouth felt dry, and a sour taste made him run his tongue over his dry lips. He needed water.

"Is there somewhere I can get a drink of water?"

"Yeah, in the hall outside men's room is a water dispenser. It's down the hall to the right. I'm going to snag forty winks in the chair in my office. You can use the AD's office two doors down from mine. I'm sure he won't mind."

"Isn't he using it?"

She shook her head. "He's missing along with rest of the agents I work with. They were deployed at the Onyx Corporation building."

"Oh…sorry," said Todd with a shake of his head.

His eyes were cast downward at the burgundy carpet. More death to add to his guilt.

"Yeah," she said, as she went out the door. Her footsteps echoed in the empty hallway until they finally receded to an empty silence.

The overhead air conditioning vents lining the parameter walls came alive in the silence of the empty boardroom to whirr and blow cold air down on him.

He shivered.

He left the room, turned right, and found the door marked "men's room" two doors down. He went inside and found the water dispenser inset into the wall. This was the purified kind, that used the city sewer water, treated it then recycled it to the core buildings in the city.

True fresh water cost a small fortune; only the upper strata of society could afford the luxury of fresh water anymore. Todd despised the local stuff.

He found the odd, metallic aftertaste disturbing. When he was a kid he'd enjoyed fresh stream water at his parent's cabin on Mackinaw Lake.

He filled a plastic glass he found in a dispenser tube next to the water spigot and was about to put the half filled glass to his lips when he hesitated.

Where were Mike's parents from? He vaguely recalled from the press reports they were from some place in Texas. Or was it Georgia? No, definitely Texas. He grunted. No one was from Texas anymore.

He took a swig of the tepid water, wrinkled his nose in disgust, then poured the rest down one of the sinks. A few hours' sleep would do him a world of good.

Mike's family...they had a house in Texas...

Pulling a paper towel from the dispenser on the wall next to the sink he used it to wipe his face. He stared at the bloodshot-eyed man staring back at him. The circles under his sagging, black-rimmed eyes made him think he was looking at someone else. His normally smooth head was covered in gray stubble.

He rubbed his chin; pity he had no time to shave.

Gazing at himself in the mirror over the sink, his face suddenly paled when a terrible scenario occurred to him. His heart rate increased. Oh, crap. Texas. That had to be it.

Tossing the empty glass in the waste bin near the door, he left the washroom at a run. Bursting into the hallway he raced down the hallway to Angela's office.

He found her curled in her chair, her arms wrapped around her slim body. She was snoring lightly.

Hesitating for a moment he watched her shoulders rise and fall in time to her breathing. Maybe this could wait.

He shook his head. No, it can't wait. Lives were at stake.

He bent over her, placing one hand on her left shoulder and shook her gently.

"Angela?" he whispered. He shook her harder when she didn't respond. "Angela?" he said louder this time.

"What?" she said, clearly annoyed at having been woken from such a deep slumber.

Rolling over just enough, she opened one eye to a slit to gaze at him standing over her.

"What is it?" she murmured.

"I know where we'll find Mike."

That caught her attention.

Angela shifted her weight in the chair and yawned. Blinking her eyes open she squinted at him from the sudden intrusion of light even though it was subdued.

Todd shifted his feet; something had made him vaguely uncomfortable, though he didn't know why.

"So?" she said after several seconds of silence. "I'm listening."

"Texas," he said finally, his voice trembling with anxious excitement.

"Why Texas?"

"Wasn't that where he was born?"

She nodded. "Yeah, so what?"

"If I remember correctly, his parents kept him off the citizen rolls. He didn't get the legally required transmitter implant when he was born. That's why you guys were unable to track him. I seem to recall they lived in Texas. I think it makes sense he'd go back there."

Angela sat up, unfolded her legs as a cat might, then placed her bare feet on the carpeted floor. She had removed her shoes for her nap, and her white cotton blouse was untucked from her suit pants. Her rumpled appearance reminded him she was human after all. Up to now she'd seemed so stiff and uptight.

Her normally buoyant hair lay flat on her head. She gazed at him saying nothing. Her eyes said she was running over possibilities in her head.

Finally she said, "The Sikes family, though we don't even know if that's their real name — the whole diseased clan is off the radar. They lived in a few different towns in Texas. They were nomads after the great social and economic upheavals in 2016.

"Besides, Road, the Texas territory is off-limits. The barrier project keeps the majority of the state fenced-off. Marauders control the towns and villages now; it isn't even a real state anymore. And the old cities are abandoned radioactive waste dumps."

Todd nodded. "Mike would have no problem getting inside with the aliens' help. And he knows we won't follow him. What's a more perfect place?"

"Yeah," she said slowly. "You might be right."

Then she added, "Let's get a couple of hours' shut-eye, then check with GIANT to see what towns Mike and his family lived in. We'll pick the most likely one from that list. We'll need a plan to get in and out before the marauders discover us. They have their own fiefdoms down there, and the local Warlords don't take too kindly to visitors."

Todd trembled at the thought. He'd heard the stories.

Angela curled her legs back under her lithe body and rolled over to face the back of the chair curled back into a ball. She began to snore as soon as her head hit the arm rest. How does she do that?

He stared at her for several seconds unable to speak. This was crazy. What the hell was he thinking going into the no-man's-land? Texas was the most deadly place on Earth, a human meat grinder.

SEVENTEEN

MIKE GAZED DISPASSIONATELY at the young woman hanging by her outstretched arms from the sturdy-looking beams in the ceiling. Her bare, dirty feet dangling in the stale air of the moldy, damp cellar.

Azelia Marks, her strawberry blonde hair buzz cut, her left eye swollen and an angry shade of purple. She was unconscious, though that was about to change.

Her faded blue jeans and black tee-shirt were streaked with the. He had dragged her limp body across the overgrown, weed-marred yard, pulling her from the alien shuttle to the house.

God, she's plain.

Flat breasts, wide hips, almost no womanly form to her at all. It was like she was a man in a woman's body. He'd thrown away the worn, tanned boots she'd been wearing when he snatched her, because they made her too manly as far as he was concerned.

In the flickering light from the candles set around the room on stumps and the rickety sticks of furniture, he smirked as he gazed upon her. Pal had extinguished the light he'd brought with him when Mike lighted the candles.

The flickering of the golden flames made his prey seem to move even though she was suspended from the heavy oak beam.

He'd tied a gag made of a soiled rag over her mouth.

Not that screaming would do any good in this remote shack.

He'd tied her bare feet together with a short length of clothesline cord he'd found in the oily scraps of cloth piled about haphazardly in the damp cellar.

He gazed at her and wondered what punishment she deserved. She was going to die, that much was certain, but how? He'd killed using so many methods over the years that no one was his personal favorite.

He glanced at Pal who stood watching, his face impassive. He wasn't going to interfere. In fact Pal seemed anxious to see what he'd do next.

"So what do you think, my alien friend? How should I do her?"

Pal's red eyes gazed back at him. The alien mimicked a motion of a knife slashing the throat that he must have seen while he observed human behavior.

Mike grinned and his eyes narrowed. A good idea to be sure, but he had something far more sinister in mind. Something he really enjoyed.

He shifted his gaze back to the unconscious woman. He moved to a small wooden table that he'd set up earlier beside her. The rotted wood and the wobbly legs made the table unsteady, but he set a car battery picked up during a nocturnal visit to an old scrap yard along with a pair of red jumper cables on the table. The current would make this entertaining and he could watch Azelia suffer before she died. He relished the idea of what was about to happen. He hoped the alien enjoyed the experience as much as he did.

The contacts on the cables were rusted almost beyond saving. Using some machine oil, and a little elbow grease, Mike managed to clean them of enough rust to make them useable, and connected one end to the battery.

Fortunately, some of the older farmers around here still used gasoline-driven tractors and other combustion vehicles, so fully-charged car batteries were still available. He liked to wake his victims with a shock.

He lifted the jumper cables and attached the red, positive cable to one of Azelia's booted feet with a large greasy alligator clip. He then lightly tapped her bare left arm with the negative clip, and watched her body jerk as the voltage traveled through her unconscious form.

Her eyes popped open with surprise. She emitted a muffled cry of pain, eyes searching wildly for relief as she looked up the length of twisted rope above her head to see it hung over the beam. She began to struggle against her bonds.

"I wouldn't do that if I were you," said Mike in an even tone. "I've poured water over those ropes. The more you struggle the more they'll tighten."

Azelia ceased her struggle and her ebony complexion paled as she gazed at him. She hung limp as a rag doll swinging gently to and fro from her attempt to free herself. She began to sob, and large tears began to run down her dusky, pudgy cheeks.

He ran the end of the alligator clip over her bare arm again, and again she jerked, her eyes widened with pain. She made a strangled cry through the oily cloth gag.

Mike moved a metal-framed kitchen chair with a ripped brown leatherette seat beside her then stood up on it so that he was at eye level with her. Her expressive dark eyes looked back at him. He relished the fear in them.

A thrill of excitement ran through his body at seeing her this way. The first time he'd had her strung up like a chicken ready for slaughter, she'd given him a look of defiance. This time was different. She would have to respect him more than the first time.

He liked that. His thin lips curled in a smile. He reached over and removed her gag.

"It's okay, Azelia, no one will hear you so you can make all the noise you want. This time you won't be going anywhere. At least until we've settled our business." He stepped down to the dirt-covered floor.

"Please..." she said, her voice broken by a moaning plea.

He shook his head. "No, Azelia, my darling you've been a bad girl. You have to be punished." He looked at Pal who was watching intently from the edge of the candlelight. Pal stepped closer.

The red-eyed alien, his arms at his side, gazed at Azelia, reminding Mike of someone studying a fly caught in a spider's web.

Azelia looked down at the alien standing below her. Her eyes narrowed. "You gots a new friend," she said her words slurred slightly.

"Yes, Azelia. This is Pal. He's an alien from another world. He's helping me to tie up some loose ends before I go with them to their world."

She blinked as if she were about to pass out. "Funny looking guy for a little green man," she said.

"They think I'm a God," Mike said with evident pride.

Azelia smirked and her head lolled to one side.

"Don't smirk, Azelia. You know I don't joke. You will respect me this time."

During their last encounter she'd made the mistake of not taking him seriously, as if her were joking with her. The angry scars on her back were reminders of the missing skin he'd extracted from her to punctuate his point. Mike detested being humored by anyone, especially a victim.

He held the alligator clip closer to her. With a blank expression on his face he touched her bare arm again.

Her scream echoed off the rough log walls as she kicked against the leg restraints and her wrists twisted in the ropes.

Her arms and legs were red with blood from where the restraints were rubbing the skin raw. Trickles of dark red blood began to travel down her arms. At the same time her bladder and bowels let go simultaneously, filling the room with the smell of urine and feces.

Mike looked at Pal. "Ironic isn't it that 'Azelia' means spared by Jehovah in Hebrew? What do you think? Should I spare her?"

Pal again shrugged. The decision was his.

Pal was full of surprises. The ship was hidden behind a cloak of invisibility Pal had set up to guard it while they were inside. He was constantly pulling rabbits out of the hat just at the right moment. If Mike didn't know better, he might think the aliens were stringing him along.

He dismissed the thought.

So far they'd been his benefactors, protecting him from every threat as he went about his God-given task. But, then again, to them he was a God, so maybe he had every right to take charge of who lived and who died all by himself. Maybe when this was over he'd rule their world, and make these decisions for them as well.

Mike crossed his arms over his chest and stroked his chin with his long narrow fingers as he studied Azelia's barely conscious form. She moaned softly, her eyes closed.

A noise from outside made him stiffen. Someone was out there. Someone had invaded his territory.

There was a thump on the ceiling above their heads accompanied by booted footsteps.

Mike glanced at Pal. "We've got company."

***

Angela and Todd drove through Raisin, Cat Spring, and Zapata before finally arriving at Pumpville, an abandoned ghost town.

It was the last known place Mike's family had lived in Texas. The marauders didn't come here because it was considered haunted and a cursed place. Superstition made a perfect cover for the Sikes family. They'd lived in an old rancher's house, in seclusion from the rest of the technology-based world, protected from the frequent dust storms and the desert heat, and unmolested by the marauders' ravaging of the rest of the Texas countryside.

Mike's first victims were his mother, father, and two sisters, all killed when he was seventeen. Their DNA was found in graves in the cellar beneath the old house. At least that's who the authorities thought was buried there.

The family didn't exist according to official records. They lived off the grid. There weren't many Texans in the official records anymore, so this wasn't particularly unusual.

The Texas National Security Office border guards had been reluctant to grant Todd and Angela permission to cross the barricade into Texas until Angela showed them her FBI credentials. They were eventually granted travel authorizations for the Texas zone, but not before Angela and Todd each signed waivers to release the authorities from any responsibility for their safety while in the zone, in the event they were captured by marauders.

Todd signed the release, wondering what he'd done by suggesting they come here. The place was dangerous and he could be killed.

Angela activated the air car's defensive systems before they entered the zone, enveloping the exterior of the vehicle in armored shields. The shields would easily deflect small arms fire, but it would be put to the test by anti-air missile attack — According to the TNSO intelligence officer who'd briefed them, some of the more techno-literate marauders were rumored to have such weapons.

The air car also contained two anti-personnel gun batteries, one that rose from the hood in front and one from the rear. They would each swivel at ninety degree angles once they acquired a target. The auto tracking system would follow the target, and the gun operator — Angela on the nose gun, and Todd on the rear gun — would authorize the system to attack via verbal command.

Once activated only the two of them would have access to the verbal command control systems of the guns until the interface was reset by specially trained technicians back at the FBI's maintenance department. This would prevent an enemy from using the voice-command systems to turn the guns on their owners.

As a further safeguard, if an unauthorized person managed to get control of the air car, the vehicle would ask for an authorization code, which only Angela knew. If the code was not given correctly, the car would self-destruct in thirty seconds.

As they made their way across Texas, they didn't encounter any living persons until they came to Raisin, where a small band of marauders fired a few shots from small arms as they passed the outskirts of the town.

According to the FBI file, the Sikes had lived just outside Raisin until Mike was six, when they'd moved away as the level of tension in the old state had risen along with an increased level of violence. Scans showed no sign of life in the home; Angela and Todd moved on.

Cat Spring, a once a peaceful town, had been reduced to piles of rubble. Strategic air bombardment by the Mexicans during the border skirmish of 2023, when the Mexican Emperor attempted to annex the state, had virtually leveled this area. The Emperor's public execution a few years later ended the dream of a new Mexican Empire.

There were no houses in Cat Spring, and therefore no lair for Mike to hide.

As they moved through Zapata, it was a different story. The Zapatans must have been advised that he and Angela were coming, because they were met by heavy flak that struck the air car like hail on a tin roof.

Angela swerved and drove in a wild series of evasive maneuvers making Todd's stomach scream in protest. He pressed his hands against the car's airframe to steady himself as Angela concentrated from behind the pilot's controls.

She tagged a few flak gun posts on the ground with the nose gun. Todd managed to shoot down two interceptor missiles as they approached from behind.

Finally, they made their way to the small house just outside town listed in the file as another of the Sikes' family's homes, and their scans showed it was devoid of life. They quickly left the area followed by a trail of glowing tracer fire.

Night had fallen by the time they reached the Sikes house in Pumpville, the last Texas town recorded as a place where the Sikes family lived, and where the last of his bloodline had died. Here, body heat and DNA scans showed the house contained three distinct signatures: two male and one female. One of the males seemed to fluctuate oddly.

Angela glanced at Todd. "I think we found them."

He nodded.

“There,” she pointed at the scanner’s screen, “in the lower part of the building probably a cellar or basement of some kind.”

“Are you sure it’s them?” asked Todd, gazing at the dark ground around them.

“No, not with absolute certainty, but if you’re right about Mike bringing Azelia to Texas, this might be the perfect place for him to exact his revenge on her.”

Todd swallowed hard. Angela was right, of course, Mike couldn’t pick a more desolate or more isolated location. He mentally crossed his fingers and hoped they were in time to stop him.

There was no moon tonight; only the barest of starlight that managed to get through the polluted atmosphere lit the ground, giving it an eerie glow.

Angela turned off the car’s exterior lights to hide their presence, and engaged the silent running sequence to mask their engine noise. The dashboard controls gave off a soft green luminosity, providing the only light in the car, just enough for her to see the controls in case the auto pilot failed and they needed to make an instrument only landing.

She set the autopilot for landing and engaged the landing struts. They couldn’t use the normal landing wheels for touchdown in this rock-strewn countryside beneath them. The sensors would detect the ground cover and make the necessary adjustments to the struts to ensure a soft touchdown to lessen the risk of damage.

The last place either of them wanted to be stranded was deep in the heart of Texas.

They landed with a light bump, the car sitting on a slight downward slope, which caused it to list to the left.

Angela threw open her door and stepped onto the slope.

Todd pushed hard on his door until it opened upward then he struggled against gravity.

Angela came up to him in the gloom holding the two energy weapons she'd retrieved from the rear storage compartment. She pulled on a set of goggles, then handed Todd an identical set that he put on after adjusting the elasticized head strap so it fit correctly.

The night changed to day and he could clearly see her standing there with her gun resting on one hip. She held out a small device, which he accepted with an open palm. She motioned for him to place the device in one of his ears.

He put it in his right ear where it fit snugly.

"We'll be able to communicate this way but speak very softly. The device is very sensitive, so keep your volume low." He saw her lips move and clearly heard her voice in his ear. The device made her sound as if she was speaking in a normal conversational tone. "What about loud noises around us?" he whispered.

"It's able to filter out extraneous sounds once it's tagged your voice."

These people had more tricks up their sleeves than a poker player who cheated by stuffing cards up their shirtsleeves.

Angela nodded and began to move toward the house, which he could clearly make out at about a two hundred meters distant from where they stood. Todd hefted the heavy gun in both hands.

"Into the breach once more..." he muttered.

"No unnecessary chatter," she hissed.

He nodded then followed her.

Attached to the front of the dilapidated wooden house was a porch with broken and rotting boards, peeled paint. Using hand signals, Angela instructed him to cover the left side of the front porch. Todd didn't think the boards would hold their weight.

Angela moved forward and placed one foot gingerly on the first of three wooden steps that led up to the porch.

Todd watched her walk up the creaking steps, expecting the old wood to give way and her to fall through any second. He held his breath, fully expecting to have to leap forward and rescue the determined agent.

The odor of dry rot was thick in the air. His dry mouth already tasted of the Texas dust swirling around them in the gentle, evening breeze. Not a pleasant atmosphere for sure.

Angela made her way across the deck to the front door without incident. The front door was guarded by an outer screen door, though much of the netting was torn and shredded.

Todd followed her to stand next to the side of the door with his gun pointed at the roof extending over the front porch. The place had to be at least a hundred and fifty years old. It was a miracle it still stood.

Carefully, Angela pulled the screen door aside. It was spring-loaded and the rusted metal squeaked loudly. Angela cringed.

With the screen held back, she tested the ancient metal door handle, and after turning it halfway, they heard the latch disengage. She pushed inward, and the door opened on hinges that loudly protested the movement.

The sound of metal against metal was deafening in the silence of the evening. It struck Todd as strange that there weren't any of the night sounds you'd expect such as frogs, crickets, or other nocturnal creatures.

He took a deep breath to steady his nerves, then followed Angela inside.

They entered a room containing broken furniture discarded haphazardly about the space. The exterior windows were broken and the shredded curtains moved in the breeze that invaded the room.

The air reeked of stale cooking odors and the smell of burnt wood. Someone had been here very recently.

Todd's heart skipped a beat and he froze. Maybe they were still here.

Angela signaled to start moving again. Todd nodded, then followed her as they took up positions on opposite sides of the room, then moved through the arched doorway leading to the rest of the main floor. Here they found a hallway, containing a wooden staircase that led to the upper level, and two closed doors that led to other areas of the house.

Todd glanced at the staircase.

Angela motioned him to go first, and he made his way to the bottom of the stairs placing one booted foot on the worn burgundy carpet with a flower inlay pattern of roses and carnations covering the first step.

The step felt solid, so he began to slowly make his way up the carpeted stairs. He froze when he heard a loud crack. Suddenly the stairs beneath his feet gave way; with a loud crash, he fell through a massive hole. He stopped suddenly, jarringly, up to his waist in the middle of the rotten stairs. The dry rot had done its insidious work.

"You okay?" said Angela, staring at him from the bottom of the stairs. "Close your eyes and don't move."

A brief surge of adrenaline shot through him upon hearing her husky voice. Damn she sounded sexy. He'd never reacted to his officers in the Special Forces this way. Then again none of those guys or gals looked or talked like Angela. Must be the danger. I hope.

Todd didn't move. A sudden burst of sound startled him as a beam of energy shot from the barrel of her weapon. He shut his eyes to block out the brilliance of the light.

He opened one eye after the sound ceased. He saw she'd cut him a path. He struggled out of the hole with his elbows as the staircase around him disintegrated further.

Soon he stood next to her. Noisy, but effective.

"Thanks," he said.

She nodded. "I think they know we're here."

He grinned wryly. "You think so?" he joked.

She gave him a brief smile, which disappeared as they heard a thump, then silence. Todd couldn't decide which direction the sound came from.

He drew a breath, then held it as he strained to detect any additional sounds. Nothing.

She signaled to him they were going to investigate the origin of the sound. He nodded.

They cautiously made their way down the hallway toward the two closed doors they'd seen earlier, her leading and him following, glancing behind them occasionally in case someone suddenly appeared.

As they reached the first door they each took a side. Angela was closest to the doorknob. She reached down with one hand and turned the knob. It stopped part-way, the click of lock stopping the mechanism from working.

She signaled that she was going to kick the door in. He shook his head and mouthed it might be a trap. She shrugged and nodded.

She stepped back, and with one foot kicked the old and rotting door near the doorknob. A hole appeared, and her foot disappeared through it.

She almost lost her balance before she managed to extract it through the torn wood. She then lowered a shoulder and rushed through the door, crouching low, with her weapon at the ready.

The flimsy door was easily thrown aside. Angela burst through, then rolled across the floor coming up ready to fire from the hip with her energy rifle. Todd rushed in behind her, his rifle at the ready, searching for a target.

They were in a bathroom with an ancient, stained, white porcelain tub, resting on clawed feet in the center of the room.. A rust stain ran down the side of the tub from where the tap would normally be to the dirt-clogged drain. The drain lay on the floor, shattered into three pieces; the thin copper water pipes hung from the wall, twisted like golden spaghetti strands.

The overwhelming smell of urine and feces made Todd cover his mouth and nose.

Through the cracked glass of the window, Todd could make out the dull orange moon rising in the night sky.

The room was devoid of life.

She nodded at him and they went back into the empty hallway. "One more door," he heard her say.

This time he took the lead, kicking in the door with one booted foot. It was the cobweb-covered kitchen that had been abandoned many years before.

They moved back into the hallway just as another thump rumbled, this time clearly from underfoot.

"I don't like basements. Too easy for someone to ambush you from the dark corners," she said grimly.

He nodded as sweat formed in his armpits. But they had no choice but go into the basement. If it was Mike, they would kill him. He'd never surrender, not now that he'd been convicted and sentenced to death. Todd wondered if the aliens would follow through on their threat to destroy the Earth if they succeeded in killing Mike? Could this be end of everything?

He hoped Azelia was at least alive down there. As unlikely as that was.

They searched the remainder of the empty first floor and found a door with a darkened staircase leading down.

They peered into the darkness, but their night-vision goggles' range was insufficient to allow them to make out much of anything in the gloom.

Everything has limitations.

***

Mike moved the battered kitchen chair aside after he'd reapplied Azelia's gag then blew the candles out. On the table lay saws, knives, ice picks and other tools of his trade. All were stained reddish brown with dried blood.

His eyes quickly adjusted to the darkness. He knew this room well.

At the top of the wooden staircase the door squeaked open, followed by the sound of heavy footsteps slowly moving down the stairs one at a time. Someone was coming.

Suddenly the darkness erupted with a beam of intense white light cutting through the suffocating darkness to form a bright spotlight at the bottom of the stairs.

Pal stood impassively, watching as Mike scurried to the corner behind the staircase. Whoever it was was going to get the surprise of their shortened life when they come down here, thought Mike with a sly grin.

There were two sets of footsteps on the stairs now. The light cast by their flashlight allowed Mike to look for something to dispatch these two. He spotted an old rusted shovel standing in the corner behind him. He carefully picked it up in both hands. The weight meant it was in good enough shape to be his weapon of choice.

He smiled to himself.

First one silhouetted figure, then another reached the bottom of the stairs. The light played over Azelia dangling from the beam. Her eyes were wild now as she tried to signal they should look behind them. It'll do you no good, girl.

Mike could see by their outlines one of the two was a woman. He moved forward with the shovel raised just as Pal stepped out of the shadows. On seeing the alien suddenly appear the two figures froze where they were as if they were made of clay.

This provided Mike the opportunity he needed.

He hefted the shovel and with the steel blade he managed to cut down the two where they stood. They dropped to the floor as the heavy blade contacted with their unprotected skulls.

Mike swung it across their heads like a demented baseball player. Copper-tinted red blood spurted from their head wounds as the steel made contact with bone and flesh. This was accompanied by the sickening sound of their skulls being cracked open like ripe melons by the force of Mike's blow.

The flashlight dropped to the ground, rolled once then stopped against a pile of discarded newspapers to spray its golden beam of light over the log wall now splattered with the blood of Mike's latest victims.

EIGHTEEN

Angela pulled a flashlight from the strap on her belt beneath her suit jacket, and switched it on.

It cast a beam of golden light, just bright enough to make their night-vision goggles to be effective in the pitch-black cellar, but not as bright as a normal white light, which would have blinded their ability to see with the goggles.

The light cast by the flashlight showed a dirt floor at the bottom of the cellar stairs, dark stains near the circle of light. Todd strained to hear any movement but heard nothing.

Angela signaled she would go first and for him to follow close behind. He nodded as she moved toward the top step and began a slow descent into the dark cellar.

The ancient wooden stairs creaked with each step until they reached the bottom of the stairs. Angela began to play the light over the log walls of the trash-strewn cellar. Old cans and bottles clogged with dirt covered the floor.

From the corner of one eye, Todd detected a sudden flurry of movement and held his rifle up with both arms as someone came out of the shadows and rushed at him, holding something over its head as if to attack him.

He deflected the blow with his rifle and the attacker sprawled forward, the heavy object in the man's grip carrying him to the floor. Todd quickly brought the rifle to bear and pressed the firing stud.

A burst of white-hot energy caught the fallen figure in the center of its back and a man's voice screamed, then went silent, as the beam cut a hole the size of a basketball through him, dissolving the internal organs.

A second figure holding what looked like an axe over its head leapt from the shadows and into the beam of Angela's flashlight. He charged at her, swinging the axe wildly. She stepped back to brace herself as the man was too close for her to raise her rifle to fire in time.

Todd whirled and fired from the hip, the deadly beam catching the man in mid-torso. By the light of Angela's flashlight, Todd saw his dark eyes go wide. With a strangled cry from cracked red lips the energy beam picked him up off his feet and shoved him backward to slam against the wall of logs behind him.

He dropped to the dirt floor in a heap of smoking flesh like a puppet whose strings were abruptly cut. Todd dropped his finger from the firing stud and the rifle's deadly beam shut off.

The air reeked of stale urine and mildew, mixed with the smell of burnt flesh. A haze of smoke drifted through the beam of the flashlight.

Angela used the flashlight to survey the wreckage of their would-be attackers.

She sighed heavily as she stood up from where she'd squatted beside the charred corpse that Todd had taken out with his first shot.

"These two aren't them," she said flatly. She kicked the nearest corpse's badly deteriorated Nike's.

Two males, both men probably in their mid-thirties, although this was just a guess due to the hard existence inherent of life in the Texas dead zone. Many men and women wore rags and long scraggly, dirt-covered beards, like the ones adorning the sallow features of the dead men.

Their filthy brown hair (which might have been blond underneath the layer of caked-on grime) was matted with knots shiny with oil. What skin showed was riddled with sores common to people who suffered from malnutrition. It was unlikely they would have had the strength to take Angela or Todd, even with their makeshift weapons.

The one who lay against the wall had dropped the rust-covered axe while the man who lay face down was shrouded in smoke that rose from the large charred hole in his body like wispy fog in the morning air. Near the dead marauder lay a rusted steel shovel with a broken wooden handle.

The poor wretches must have used the last of their strength to attack them. These were desperate men on the verge of starvation.

And Todd had ended their brutal lives with two shots.

"It's okay, Road. One of them would've eventually killed the other for dinner anyway."

Todd felt his stomach twist and tasted bile at the back of his throat. Animals. Beneath this veneer of civilization we're all just animals.

She smirked. "It's for the best. You put them out of their misery. Don't sweat it." She turned and started back up the stairs to the first floor of the house.

Todd glanced back at the two crumpled corpses now barely visible in the retreating light of the flashlight.

There was a sound coming from somewhere above their heads as if the screen door upstairs was slammed against its doorframe. Angela glanced back at Todd with a worried expression on her face. She hurried up the rest of the stairs, taking two at a time.

Rest in peace. Todd gazed at the bodies of the two dead men before he turned away and rushed to follow her. His stomach churned as he climbed the stairs.

***

Mike stood over one of the bloody corpses his face calm and the rusted shovel held over his head at the ready to inflict more damage if required.

The intruders had turned out to be two locals. Paramilitary types. Marauders. Their brown-and-green uniform shirts were stained with splatters of blood, which continued to ooze from the vicious head wounds he'd inflicted. They'd be dead soon.

Mike bent over the man and grasped his right hand by the limp wrist.

He cast a steely-eyed glance at Pal, then stepped back and brought the shovel down again hard on the man's head. The flat of the shovel's metal blade hit with a resounding crack, and the body shifted slightly beneath the force of the blow.

Mike again bent down to check the pulse and nodded with a satisfied expression on his face as and let the limp wrist drop to the dirt floor.

He stepped over the man's now lifeless body and checked the woman. The bleeding from her head wound had stopped. Mike released her limp arm and let it drop into the pool of her own blood.

How disappointing. Just when I'm having fun, she up and dies on me.

He smiled thinly as he moved to stand next to the struggling figure of Azelia, whose eyes were wide with horror. Massive tears ran down her dusky cheeks. Mike thought she looked like a fish on the end of a hook.

"So, my sweet…"

Mike let the shovel slip from his fingers and fall to the dirt floor with a muffled thump. He stood in the blood of the two dead marauders.

He watched Azelia silently attempt a scream through the gag that covered her mouth and chuckled. His eyes narrowed. "Where were we before we were so rudely interrupted?" he muttered softly.

He picked up a fish-boning knife from the table and studied the partially oxidized blade. A dark red stain ran along the cutting edge.

"This looks a little dull. Why don't we sharpen it before…" Mike glanced at Pal with a smirk on his face.

Azelia struggled harder against her bonds and the room was filled with her muffled, desperate cries.

Suddenly there was another loud thump overhead. Someone else had entered the house above.

"Fuck," Mike whispered his full lips twisted in a grimace. "When will they leave me alone?"

NINETEEN

THEY'D BEEN IN the air car for an hour since leaving the dead men and the Texas Territory. Todd watched the countryside slide by below them in silence as the sky ahead of them on the horizon change to burnt oranges and reds. Dawn was coming. The farms and towns below were coming to life. Country people lived a simple way of life. Maybe he should too.

"Do you ever yearn for the simple life?" he asked as he watched a farmer walking toward his red barn from his blue and white house.

The farmer glanced at them as they went by tipping his head back as he shielded his eyes against the glare of the new day with one hand. He wore blue coveralls and a wide-brimmed tan hat. The man's face was covered with a long dark beard that seemingly extended to the top of his wide chest.

Todd felt the urge to wave, but resisted it.

Angela, her eyes scanning the sky ahead, grunted. "What the hell are you talking about now, Road?" She shook her head. "You show-biz people are dreamers. The world is a hard and scary place, that's all there is to it."

"I don't believe that, Angela…"

"Don't think because you saved my life back there, that somehow we're now buds or some shit. It's not that I'm not grateful, it's just as my unofficial partner you are expected to back me up in tight spots. I would've done the same for you."

Todd sighed heavily and nodded. "Maybe we should talk. If you have some problem with me; I'm a good listener…." Todd gazed at her with his best imitation of a wounded puppy.

She glanced over at him, her eyes fiery, but her features softened and her eyes sagged a little when she saw his expression. She struggled to contain an amused smile. It was the first time he'd seen a genuine smile from her. It looked good on her.

"Road, you are really something. We'll talk about this later. Right now we've arrived at the next map coordinates so get ready."

Todd looked around and saw they were about to land in a small town street. The one-story wooden buildings that lined the street looked to be from another era.

In earlier times the street would have been lined with wooden telephone poles, like the ones in the historical vids; but they were long-buried in the poly-alloy tunnels that crisscrossed America.

The tunnels contained all the national power grid optic cables and the communication nodes for the link that connected everyone to everyone else. The nodes were also designed to allow the government and law enforcement to track every registered person in the country. Right now the system was useless.

"If only…." mused Todd.

"What was that?" said Angela casting him an inquiring look as the air car settled on its landing gear with a bump.

"Nothing," he said hurriedly. "Where are we?"

"My home town, Grantville, Virginia," Angela said with obvious pride.

Todd looked around at the two-lane, black-topped road with the white lines that ran down the center, the fresh paint on the old buildings. A collection of the normal small town types, looking like they were right out of an old Saturday Evening Post painting he'd seen in a museum once, stared back at them as the car's engine died.

Not that Todd knew what 'normal' was anymore.

They exited the car into the fresh morning air. As they walked across the parking lot, a light breeze carried with it the scent of hay and grasses mingled with the scent of fertilizer. This was a real farming town, the bread-basket that fed America.

At least some things hadn't changed in all the social upheaval of past decades.

Todd mounted the sidewalk and nodded to some of the people as they passed them. Young women with toddlers in tow; older, grey-haired women; men wearing faded farmers coveralls, much like the farmer he'd seen from the air prior to landing. They smiled briefly as they caught his eye. He couldn't help but notice their tolerant expressions.

City folk. They'd labeled him immediately upon seeing him.

Of course, he knew they were right but somehow it still made him feel uncomfortable.

He'd somehow built up this fantasy in his mind that he was middle-America. That his talk show represented them, these people right here. Why didn't they welcome him with open arms?

Then again why should they?

Angela stopped outside a squat, one-story building with a red neon sign in the front picture window. It was the Grantville Diner.

"You hungry?" said Angela with a brief smile as her eyes flashed. She was almost human. A refreshing change from the serious FBI agent.

She held the glass and wood door open while he went inside ahead of her.

He entered, accompanied by the sound of a small, steel bell that tinkled brightly hung above the door. .

He was immediately assaulted by the smell of fresh-baked bread, which made his mouth water. He was hit by the shock of realization that even though he'd seen two people die only an hour before, he was suddenly filled with a hunger that made his stomach tighten.

When had he last eaten? He couldn't seem to remember his last meal.

Todd followed Angela to the lunch counter where took their seats on two round, metal, post-shaped stools with deep red vinyl cushions near the end of the counter.

He studied the little diner.

At one end of the pale, green-and-white counter, was a glass stand with a chocolate layer cake inside. Behind the counter, was a brown, wood, swinging door with a glass window at eye level to prevent collisions and separated the kitchen from the front of the diner. The shiny aluminum pass-through counter, through which the cook would slide the orders, was off to his left.

A middle-aged black man, wearing a tall white chef's hat, stood in the kitchen. The cook glanced up to stare at the two new arrivals through the pass-through window.

When the cook fixed his gaze on Angela, a slow, white-toothed smile spread across his dark-skinned face. His eyes lit up like a kid's on Christmas morning.

He signaled to the waitress who glanced at them then back at her ordering pad. The waitress appeared to be in her mid thirties, with blonde hair tied in a bun. She wore a plain white uniform with a pale peach apron tied round her ample waist. She walked away from them toward the excited who was waving at her to come to the pass-through counter.

Todd thought she heard him mention Angela's name and point in their direction.

Angela, for her part, sat still with her fingers overlapping as her arms rested on the counter. She had a small, knowing smile across her face. Her cheeks were flushed and she looked like a cat with a cornered mouse.

The waitress turned to focus her hazel eyes on the duo. Upon seeing Angela, her face broke into a wide smile and rushed toward them.

The glass coffee pot she was holding swayed violently in her left hand as she hurried toward them. Todd thought they might be sprayed with hot coffee. He cringed with his eyes shut as the waitress arrived, letting out a massive shout that echoed off the walls.

"Ang!" she shouted

Angela bolted from her seat and came around the counter. The waitress put down the coffee pot, and the two women embraced and both began to cry.

Todd sat silently, watching this previously cold fish of a woman sob and try in vain to speak, but her words were caught in a torrent of sobs. After several seconds the cook came out of the kitchen, and the procedure was repeated.

"It's... so good... to see you," said the cook in between crying jags.

Finally things settled down, and they separated, and Angela turned to introduce them to Todd. "Jock Carter, Leona Willis, I'd like you to meet Todd Road…"

"The Todd Road…" said the woman identified as Leona said stepping back ever so slightly.

Jock frowned at him, and Todd felt his cheeks grow warm. Here it comes. "You're the guy who helped that piece of shit, Sikes—"

"Now, Jock, Mr. Road is our guest—"

Jock pointed one index finger at Todd as he faced Angela. "You're not trying to bag Angela are ya?"

Angela laughed.

It was the first time Todd had heard Angela laugh. The sound was throaty and incredibly sexy. Today was turning out to be full of firsts.

"Not in a million years, Jock. Not if he was the last man on Earth," said Angela turning to look at Todd who now wore a slightly wounded expression.

She slapped him on the back obviously enjoying the joke at his expense. "What do ya' think there, killer? You and me against the world?"

Todd scowled and kept his mouth tight. She was making fun of him.

He looked to Jock and Leona for help. They smirked, and Jock turned and headed for the kitchen. Leona ignored him and said to Angela, "I'll go get 'im."

He who? thought Todd. Must be the busboy, He shrugged and returned to studying the menu.

Angela nodded, then plucked a menu from the aluminum holder attached to the other side of the counter between them, then returned to her seat beside him.

The glass sugar jar and the gray and white plastic salt and pepper shakers sat in front of the menu holder.

"I was a solider in the gulf y'know," said Todd under his breath in a hoarse whisper. "I don't appreciate being made a fool of."

Angela kept her eyes on the menu pages as she said, "I don't give a shit. You're an out-of-shape rookie as far as I'm concerned…."

"Stop it, Agent Cody…"

She dropped the menu on the counter, the plastic cover slapping the linoleum. She whirled in her seat and faced him, her eyes afire with intensity.

"Listen carefully, Road. You could've gotten us killed back there. You were lucky. That's all there is to it. I'm glad you shot when you did, and I appreciate you saved my life, but I don't want you to start thinking you can handle this stuff because you can't. When we meet up with Sikes and his alien pal, they're not going to be some half starved sewer rats. You got it?"

Todd glared at her, and started to say something more when she said, "Not another word. You listen to me from now on, and when I say jump, you just ask how high."

Todd leaned back in his seat and was about to offer a rebuttal, when a gray-bearded man entered the diner. He wore a blue-and-white plaid work shirt, tucked into the waistband of blue jeans that barely contained a pot belly.

A pair of wire-rimmed reading glasses was perched atop his head of long, shaggy, white hair. Wispy strands bounced off his broad shoulders. His cool, blue eyes seemed to smile in combination with his wide mouth. He seemed oddly familiar, yet Todd had never laid eyes on him before.

"Ang. I've missed you so much," said the man, throwing his arms wide around Angela.

His bear-like arms enveloped her lithe frame.

With her back to him Todd watched the big man's face as he hugged her tight, his eyes now closed. They must know each other really well.

I don't think he's the busboy.

Finally, after what seemed like an eternity, he released her, resting a meaty hand on her hip. He gazed at her with a smile on his ruddy complexion. She kept her long arms casually about his bull neck. They looked into each other's eyes with a fondness bred of familiarity.

"You don't visit nearly often enough," said the man, with a gentle scold in his gruff voice.

"I know, Dad," said Angela, her voice bright.

The man was her father. Todd didn't know what he'd expected of the man who'd sired this dedicated, tough-as-nails FBI agent, but here he was, larger than life. He looked more like a biker than a father. Todd noted that his long, shaggy, white hair. Wispy strands bounced off his broad shoulders as he turned and eyed Todd.

"I heard you scolding this young man from the back. Why don't you introduce me?"

Angela let go of her father's neck and swung around, keeping one arm laced through her father's arm, the other resting on her hip. "Milt Cody meet Todd Road..."

Milt Cody's bushy gray eyebrows arched. "Todd Road. The radio guy?" Todd nodded, fidgeting in his seat.

"Okay. Why don't we move to a booth and you tell me what's been going on. I hear some bad things are happening in the world."

Milt placed an arm around his daughter's shoulder and she pressed into his side as Todd followed on trembling legs close behind.

Milt signaled to Leona to bring them each a coffee and held up two fingers for menus, then enveloped Todd with the other bear-like arm, and guided the two of them to a secluded corner at the back of the diner, where he said they'd be undisturbed.

When they were settled in the horseshoe shaped booth, each with a steaming cup of black coffee in front of them, and Leona had gone back to the kitchen with Todd's and Angela's lunch orders, Milt said, "Now, what's goin' on?"

Milt listened intently as Angela explained what had happened to-date.

She told him about the death of her partner and the others; Mike Sikes's escape, which they suspected was engineered by the aliens; the disappearance of the FBI response force and the local cops; the chase across the country that stemmed from their review of the case file and ended with the incident in Texas and, finally their arrival here.

Leona dropped off two plates of food just as Angela finished her story.

Milt nodded grimly, then shifted his gaze to Todd. "Now why don't you explain how you got involved in this mess?"

Todd felt his stomach knot under the older man's gaze. "Huh... well... I..." he stumbled over his words. How could he explain?

"He's the cause of all this," said Angela bluntly.

Todd felt a sudden flash of anger, and glared at her with contempt. Until this moment, he'd thought they'd built a bond between them, 'comrades in arms' and all that rot.

I guess not.

"Well, sir...."

"Call me Milt. Everybody does."

"Yeah… okay… um, let's see… Mike was a frequent guest on my show—"

"Where he gave the son of a bitch a platform to spew his—" interrupted Angela.

Milt eyed his daughter sternly silencing her. She grimaced and slumped in her seat like a small child being scolded by her parent for having her hand in the cookie jar.

"Sorry, please continue," said Milt calmly.

"Huh… yeah… okay… so Mike, he called me at least once a week. I asked Amy, my producer, to make sure he got priority whenever he called. Anyway, he would call and I'd pretend…" he eyed Angela whose scowl deepened, "to go along with his loony ideas. It made for great entertainment. My ratings went way up. People are fascinated by this stuff… "

Milt cleared his throat and waved him on with a thin smile of encouragement.

"Anyway, so one day he calls and says that aliens are coming to free him. He thinks he's a God or something. Can you believe that? A mass murderer a God? I mean it's crazy except… "

"Except what?" said Milt.

Todd hesitated, his eyes drifted to his half eaten burger and fries. He stomach rumbled, but the food would have to wait.

"Mike is a smart guy and certainly not crazy — psychopathic, yeah, but not crazy — so I should have taken his warning seriously. But who'd have thought aliens… " He hesitated. It must sound as if he'd lost his mind.

"Anyway," he continued, "The aliens came — and they took me to their ship in Earth's orbit where they communicated with me telepathically." Todd raised his hands as if in surrender. "I know it all sounds loony, but it's true I swear."

Milt glanced at Angela with his white eyebrows raised. Angela shrugged and rolled her eyes.

"Are you in communication with them now?" asked Milt. At the edge of his- voice, Todd thought he heard the skepticism of someone who thought he was, indeed, losing his grip on reality.

"No. I asked Pie — that's the head alien, as best as I could make it out, their names are long and unpronounceable so I shortened them up — to stop talking inside my head." Todd continued his story. "So Pal, that's the other alien, brought me back and we took Mike to my studio for an interview. It was during the interview that the world went to hell."

"Do you think you could get this 'Pie' to speak inside your head again?" Milt eyed the talk show host; his large, meaty fingers combing through his neatly -rimmed white beard.

"Maybe, at least I think so. It's not like turning on a radio, but I can ask him. I think he'll probably respond, he has before," Todd said slowly, his eyes drifted to Angela. Her brow was wrinkled and her arms were crossed over her chest.

Milt placed one massive arm across his daughter's shoulders, his features gentle with a knowing grin.

"Now, now, my little girl; we have a tool sitting right in front of us far better than that old GIANT system of yours."

Angela's eyes shifted to Todd. "Ex-military Intel," she said with a shrug. "Dad knows all sees all."

Todd grinned.

Ignoring his daughter, Milt Cody locked eyes with Todd. "We may have just found the key to the kingdom." Milt's eyes narrowed. "And I hope the aliens will cooperate or we may all suffer."

TWENTY

MIKE WENT OVER TO the two corpses of the snoopy marauders and retrieved the pistols that lay in the pools of blood surrounding their cooling bodies.

He wiped the butts of their nine-millimeter Glocks with a scrap of an old, ragged towel he'd found in a pile of rotting cloth in one corner of the room. These pretend soldiers are getting some nice guns these days.

Then, gripping the men's automatic pistols in each hand, he moved to the bottom of the stairs and paused to hold his breath; straining to listen to the sounds of the footsteps coming from above their heads. Pal stood beside him.

"There are three," said Pal in his emotionless tone.

Mike turned his head sideways and tossed the alien a crooked smile, his eyes narrowed. "Yeah," he said. "It's gonna be a hell of party."

Mike went back over to the struggling Azelia, lifted the charged alligator clips to one bare arm, and shocked her into unconsciousness.

She hung limp, like a rag doll, with her arms straight above her head and her chin resting on her chest, her eyes closed. Her chest moved with each shallow breath, so he hadn't killed her. Yet.

Good, we'll play later, my darling.

Starting up the stairs, he was careful to pause at each step in order to detect any change in the footsteps coming from above. He didn't want them to hear him coming. They'd start looking below soon enough.

Surprise was his weapon, and he would need plenty of it if he was going to get out of this one. Wouldn't Cody be pleased if he were caught again? Maybe the Texas militia kill me this time. He smirked to himself. Yeah, right.

Finally, he reached the top of the stairs. Pal followed close behind imitating his every gesture.

Mike had long ago convinced himself murder was a benefit to humanity. Without crime, life would be dull and uninteresting. Perhaps it was his destiny, maybe his job even, to show these aliens the benefits and the power experienced by a human committing murder.

Mike handed one of the pistols to Pal. With a series of hand gestures he showed the alien where the deadly end was and how the trigger worked.

What he didn't do was remove the safety. He didn't want the alien to make the mistake of shooting him.

A rush of adrenaline accompanied his opening the trap door a crack. A figure dressed in a Texas militia uniform different from the two bodies lying at the bottom of the stairs flashed past by the door without seeing him. Unlike the dead marauders the new intruders were professionals. Mike smiled to himself. He relished the challenge.

Listening intently he heard the footsteps from three pairs of boots. They sounded as if they were farther away from the trap door> He then pressed his shoulder into the trap door and it swung open.

Climbing up the ladder into the main room he waited as Pal followed close behind then eased the trap door shut trying not to make any noise as it closed.

Once in the hallway, Mike and Pal pressed themselves flat against the wall and Mike held the pistol pointed upward in front of him.

Stepping sideways, spider-like, they made it to the corner where two walls converged. Mike stole a quick glance around the corner and saw one uniformed militia.

His tan, Boy Scout-style hat sat forward on his closely-cropped hair, exposing the bristles of his brown crew-cut. The cop was whispering into an old-fashioned device Mike recognized as a portable communicator called a walkie talkie. He'd never seen one, but had read about them while in prison in an article about the history of communication.

He needed to time this just right.

Stealing a glance around the corner, Mike heard the cop whisper he was signing off then going to search the lower floors.

His body in a tight crouch, Mike moved rapidly toward the cop on the tips of his toes, hoping to lessen the sound as he crossed the distance between them like a cat.

The militia man started to turn as Mike came up behind him. Mike lifted the pistol, butt down, and hit him hard at the top of his spine at the base of the neck.

The man fell forward, landing hard on his face with a loud smack. It sounded like a fish being landed by a fisherman.

He lay still. Grinning, Mike turned to look at Pal who'd moved from behind the wall, his pistol still aimed at the ceiling.

Mike tensed when he heard shouts coming from outside the house. Suddenly the door burst open and two uniformed militia rushed into the room, their guns at the ready.

Pal, his face free of emotion, dropped them with one shot each from his pistol. The bullets struck them each in the center of their foreheads and the momentum of their rush to get into the room caused them to drop and slid across the floor, their corpses stopping at Pal's feet. Their guns clattered loudly as they fell to the floor beside their lifeless bodies.

Mike gazed at his alien friend, stunned into silence by what he'd just witnessed. The alien had somehow turned off the safety on the gun. Good thing, he mused, or I'd probably be dead.

"Did I do it right?" asked Pal, with a sloppy grin on his face like a kid with a new toy.

Mike nodded, his voice barely above a whisper, "Yeah. Good." They'd bury the bodies with the dead marauders. A surge of excitement passed through Mike. How he loved his work.

TWENTY ONE

Milt Cody smiled thinly, his pale gray eyes studying Todd as if he were under a microscope.

The smirk on Angela's pretty face told him he wasn't going to be able to back out of this. He didn't want the aliens inside his head again — the echo of their voices inside his brain made his head hurt.

Maybe human brains weren't compatible to alien brain waves or something. All he knew was that the voices inside his head made him feel nauseous and jumpy. He hated the feel of them.

Beads of perspiration beaded his forehead and the butterflies took flight in his stomach. "I really do have to pee," he said.

Milt silently nodded toward the front of the diner. Angela chuckled briefly.

Milt's eyes narrowed. "Ya know... something about your story puzzles me," he said slowly.

Todd thought he could see the wheels turning in the older man's head. "But you go take a piss and we'll talk about it some more when you get back, okay?"

Todd nodded and rose from the booth. The vinyl-covered seat squeaked as he moved until he stood and headed toward the front of the diner where a small black and white wooden sign hung over washroom doors.

He entered the men's room and immediately collapsed against the wall.

The pressure caused by recent events had begun to crowd his mind and finally had taken their emotional toll. He was dizzy and confused. With one hand pressed against the wall he launched himself toward the twin white porcelain sinks.

He stumbled across the urine-stained floor that smelled like it must have been recently bleached to the nearest sink, turned on the cold water, and splashed some in his face. He rested both hands on the counter on either side of the sink and looked up to gaze at his drawn, haggard face.

He hadn't shaved in two days, and salt-and-pepper stubble dotted his face. The dark circles under his eyes made him look old.

He moved across the room to the urinal, did his business, then stumbled back to the sink to wash his hands.

Glaring at himself in the mirror, he straightened, pushing back his shoulders thereby adjusting the line of his jacket. He cleared his throat. His mouth tasted like it was full of cotton.

He wasn't about to show these two any weakness. Not now. Not after all he'd been through. He would contact Pie, get of Mike Sikes' location, and then he and Agent Cody would take the bastard out.

Yup, that was it. That's what he'd do — the right thing — for a change. Ratings be hanged.

He made his way back to the table, though his legs were like rubber. Maybe this wasn't a good idea after all; false bravado and all.

He went to sit down across from Milt Cody, who was talking softly to his daughter. She seemed to be hanging on his every word. When Todd plunked himself down, they abruptly stopped talking.

"Well, don't you look better," said Milt with a glance at Angela who smiled wickedly.

"Yeah. I feel better, too," said Todd easing his tired, aching back against the high-backed, overstuffed vinyl cushion behind him.

"Not so fast there, cowboy. We need to talk about something — something Angela and I have been talking about since you left. I want to see if you draw the same conclusion. Okay?"

Todd nodded.

"Have these aliens blown up anyone else that you know of, except outside the Onyx Corporation building?"

"Huh… they made the FBI tactical team disappear…"

Milt nodded. "Exactly."

Todd frowned and Angela, seated across from him now, smiled, her eyes showing her admiration for her father. She emulated the man, that much was clear.

"No…I guess not. At least not that we know of"

Milt slapped the table, which made Todd start. "Exactly," said Milt, his gray face split in a wide grin. "Ang, I believe the man's got it." Milt paused and he became serious, his eyes visibly darkening. "I think you're being played."

"I agree. So far the aliens are protecting Mike Sikes by eliminating people who interfere with their plans," Todd said. "I just had trouble believing them." He realized he should have believed them, but too many lies, too many people playing games made him doubt anyone or any being.

Milt waved one hand casually in Todd's direction as he eased back against the seat cushion. "See I told ya, Ang, he's got it."

"What do we do?" said Todd.

Angela, her expression now serious leaned toward him. "I think once they've finished with him, they'll kill Sikes." She held up one hand to stop Todd's protestations.

"I don't know how I know let's just say my well tuned FBI gut is telling me and we we'll leave it at that. Only we have to find him before they off the son if a bitch."

Todd gazed at her perplexed. "But I thought you wanted Mike dead?"

"I do, but within the confines of the law. I want the final crack at that animal, he doesn't deserve extraterrestrial justice, Earth-bound justice must prevail. Unless..." She and Milt glanced at each other, sending each other a clear message. "...Mike attempts to escape and I have no choice. If that happens, I'll take him down faster than you can say 'shit.'"

Milt smiled thinly and nodded. Obviously he agreed with his daughters well tuned gut.

"When do we start?" asked Todd.

"First things first, we need you to make contact with the alien in the ship orbiting Earth," said Angela, as if it was a simple as using a link.

Todd grimaced. "Okay." He closed his eyes and thought about Pie.

The image of the floating, glowing ball of energy leapt into his conscious mind. He saw the ball sparkling with its eerie, inner light as if it were throbbing with life, which, in fact, it was.

Hello, Mr. Road, came the voice inside his head. It was Pie.

Todd opened one eye a crack to find Milt and Angela studying him closely, as if he were an insect. A trickle of cold sweat ran down his back, under his shirt. It tickled, but he didn't feel like laughing.

He nodded at them and closed his eyes tight again. This business of talking to someone who wasn't here with them seemed ridiculous, especially with two people staring at you. Concentrate, Road, they're depending on you.

Who is? asked Pie. He sounded curious.

"Never mind, it's not important," Todd said.

"He's talking to the alien right now," Angela whispered to her father.

"What are they talking about?" asked Milt.

"Shut up. He hears everything you say before you say it." Todd gritted his teeth and his face grew warm.

Milt and Angela became silent.

"Sorry, Pie, just two rude humans interrupting our private conversation. That ever happen to you?"

Todd tried to sound as nonchalant as possible so the alien wouldn't pursue the matter further.

He heard Pie sigh heavily. Yeah. All the time. Unfortunately no one knows how to listen anymore.

This alien sounded almost human in his reactions. Todd shook off the sensation. "There's something important I need to ask you."

Oh?

"Yeah…well…you see we need to know where Mike Sikes is. You see he…"

You want to stop him.

Todd was relieved, Pie understood.

"Huh…yeah. He's captured someone and is holding her hostage. He's probably torturing this person as we speak, and will very likely kill her…"

I should hope so.

Todd stomach muscles tightened. This wasn't good. He didn't like the underlying casual tone in Pie's voice. "Huh…what do you mean?"

"Ask him about Sikes's location. Hurry…." said Angela her voice urgent.

Todd's eyes flew open and he glared at Angela. She stopped and stared at his angry features, shock registering on her pretty face. The worm had finally turned.

He closed his eyes again his forehead wrinkled in concentration. "Please explain, Pie, I'm trying to understand."

There was a long pause during which Todd was aware of the odors of the food and drink sitting untouched on the table. The milk warming in Milt's glass, the coffee that had grown cold in front of Angela, his own glass of soda gone flat with its syrupy sweet smell. His mouth was dry and he thought about taking a sip from his glass except that he detested flat soda.

It's difficult to explain…

"Why?"

Do you believe in God, Mr. Road?

"I guess so…why?"

Have you ever met him, or her?

"Of course not," Todd said, shocked by the direction this conversation was headed.

What if I told you you could meet and talk to God. That you could make your world into a home for God. One so perfect that he'd be happy to stay.

"You're not telling me you think Mike Sikes is God?"

No, not God, but the catalyst for God to come to your planet and cleanse it of evil. We've studied your religions, and found the common thread that binds them is vengeance. God comes to rectify evil. Mike Sikes's is evil so it follows God will come here. He's going to come here and wipe the Earth clean, just as he's done before.

When? Todd thought. Out loud he said, "But what has that got to do with you?" This situation was getting beyond weird.

We need a Mike.

"You want to take him with you? Well, be my guest..."

"No!" Angela cried. His eyes flew open to see her being restrained by Milt.

"Ang, no. If they want him let them have...." Todd held up both hands to stop their verbal wrestling.

I didn't mean we'd take him to our planet. He'd never survive the voyage. No human would be able to survive our technology.

"What then?"

Mike Sike's DNA will be added to the Vel'Tan you call Pal. He will be first of a new race. Once we return him to our planet, Pal will start to act like Mike Sikes and God will come. We will meet our creator, and He will stay with us forever. After we're finished you can have Mike back. But for now, we need to learn more from him.

Todd's eyes went wide and he stared at Milt and Angela, his mouth hung open. "Oh, my God..." he whispered.

Exactly.

"What...?" said Milt his voice level. Todd stared back at the older man, unable to speak.

"I think he's in shock," said Angela as she leaned forward to place one pale hand on Todd's forehead while examining first one unseeing eye then the other.

Todd shook her off. "They're trying to capture God..."

***

"You better explain," said Milt, his voice harsher, and his eyes narrowed in anger.

"They want Mike's DNA...." Todd stopped himself.

If the public knew the extent of what the aliens were planning, they might cause a panic.

Todd realized the Pel'Tac were using Mike as a catalyst to their own evolution.

He realized from his conversation with Pie that the Pel'Tac had no concept of murder or what it meant to kill. They had no idea of the evil they were about to bring down on themselves.

"You okay?" said Angela with concern evident in her voice.

"Huh... yeah..." he muttered, "just feeling a little lightheaded, that's all..." he chuckled to himself.

The telepathic contact had drained him. Since this was probably how they transmitted instructions to the Vel'Tan, he wondered if the mental contact had a similar effect on them.

He had discovered something important in the mental contact with Pie, the Pel'Tac didn't have words for murder, kill, or psychopath.

"They want to learn how to kill," Todd suddenly blurted to a startled Angela and Milt. They glanced at each other knowingly.

They must think I'm mad.

"Why?" said Angela glaring at him.

Todd hesitated, his mouth open.

"Com'on, Road, everyone, even beings from another planet, has reasons. Why do the little green men want to learn how to kill?"

"They want God to come to them."

Milt sighed heavily. "You said that before, but how is learning to kill gonna make God come to them? That doesn't make sense."

"I know it sounds crazy, Mr. Cody, but they want Mike to teach Pal how to kill then have him go on a killing spree, like Mike, on their planet. You see they believe God will come here and cleanse our world for Mike's deeds, and they want the same to happen on their planet — so they plan to meld his DNA with the Vel'Tan to create a new race. A race that is capable of murder."

"Armageddon…" whispered Angela. "I think I understand. Tell me if I'm off-base: they want this new race of serial-killer Vel'Tan's so God can destroy them and then stay with the Pel'Tac?"

"Huh… yeah… I guess so…"

"That's crazy…" said Milt.

Todd made a circular motion with his right index finger over the table that separated them. "The three of us may agree, but they don't see it that way."

"Tell them they're wrong," said Milt.

"And if you believed you could make God appear, wouldn't you want that opportunity? Even if it sounds a little nuts and is ridiculous?"

The three gazed at each other. What do you say to such an absurd situation?

Finally Angela said, "They must be nuts. We have all kinds of evil and God never showed up for us. There are days I wish He would." She shook her head. Todd stared at her his eyes quizzical. "Never mind," she said. "Ask Pie where Mike is right now and I'll go get him."

Todd shook his head. "Sorry, Angela, Pie won't help us to find him. They want to finish what they started first; then they say we can have Mike."

"But what about Azelia Marks?"

Todd shrugged.

Angela's face darkened. "You mean she has to die… ? I don't fucking think so… "

As she rose from behind the table, Todd felt a sudden urge to flee. Her eyes were on fire with an inner resolve he'd not seen in her before. He thought he'd seen her angry before but she must have been only mildly annoyed. He cringed inside as she grabbed him by the left arm and dragged him out of his seat.

She held him close, her hands gripping both of his arms now, as she said, her voice an animalistic growl, "You tell them I won't let him kill Azelia. She's an innocent who's alive today because she's the gutsiest person who ever lived…you tell them if Mike kills her I'll be coming after them next…"

"O-kay…" Todd gulped.

"Ang, take it easy. It's not his fault…"

She turned her burning eyes to her father. "Dad, stay out of this."

Milt shrugged. He obviously knew enough to heed her words. Angela was a woman who took no nonsense from anyone, including her father. Todd would try, that was the least he could do. He only hoped he'd succeed. Right now, though, the odds of keeping Azelia Marks alive were between nil and zero.

TWENTY TWO

MIKE STOOD BACK and admired his handy work. Pal shooting the cops had unnerved him at first, until he realized that the alien was imitating him, which was perfectly understandable.

A surge of pride made him realize he was setting an example for an alien culture. These beings had a lot to learn, and he was just the man to teach them.

He gazed at Azelia's bloody form hanging limply from the beam by her tied wrists. He'd been careful to remove just the top layer of her dark flesh. As with most flayings, she'd screamed until she'd passed out from the blood loss, and finally died.

Too bad, really, he enjoyed his victim's screams of agony when he killed them using such a slow, methodical technique. For Azelia, he'd chosen a finely sharpened mule-skinner's knife that he'd stolen from a museum outside Pittsburgh twenty years previous. He'd carefully made thin incisions along her skin, then slowly peeled the layer of skin in strips, leaving a trail of blood that ran down her body.

The blood pooled beneath her as she screamed and writhed in pain. The slightly metallic odor of the drying liquid on the dirt floor as it spread beneath her like coagulating tidal ponds devoid of life permeated the room.

He smiled at her lifeless corpse, her chin pressed against her chest. Her unseeing eyes were open wide just as they'd been the moment she drew her last breath.

Pal stood off to the side watching the meticulous work as Mike completed each section. The strips of blood-soaked flesh sat in a pile to one side of the twisting corpse.

His work was done. He'd taught Pal how to kill slowly and with malice aforethought.

"You understand?" Mike asked, his attention on the twisting body of the late Azelia Marks.

"Yes," said Pal's calm voice.

Mike caught the motion of something coming toward him from just outside the field of his vision, but was too late to move as he felt a burning pain, then blackness took him.

***

"She's dead."

Todd almost stopped himself before he said the words, but he couldn't help himself.

The image inside his head was so shocking, he blurted it out without thinking. His mind filled with the image of a barely-recognizable Azelia Marks, soaked in blood, hanging from a wooden beam suspended by knotted ropes. Pie supplied the image without elaboration.

Angela looked at him with a fierce expression, her face flushed and her forehead wrinkled by a scowl. He thought for a second she would hurt him. She let go of his arms and pushed him into the booth's seat. He landed hard with a grunt.

"Damn you," she said. She didn't necessarily mean him, but he wasn't certain either.

"We should go to Mike's lair." he said his voice barely above a whisper.

She whirled on him. "You know where she is? Why didn't you tell me before…"

"I didn't know until just now…"

She scowled at him, her gaze boring through him as Milt said, in a level tone, "Ang, you and Road go get her and find that son of a bitch..

Angela sighed and faced her father. "Sorry, Dad. You know what that woman's life meant to me…" She hung her head, and Todd thought for a moment she was going to start to cry. Instead her look of determination returned. When she looked up, she cast him a fierce gaze.

"Okay, Road, we're outta here."

Leaving Milt staring after them, they headed out of the diner. Todd wasn't sure he wanted to go with her, but he knew he didn't have a chance to say so. When Angela Cody made up her mind, everyone around her was expected to fall in line.

He could have said no, but Milt, had whispered to him urging him to listen to his daughter. Todd suspected he didn't want her to face Mike alone.

He chugged after her until they stood next to the air car. "You'll be driving, Road. You know where we're going, and I need time to prepare."

He headed for the driver's side while Angela opened the trunk and accessed the weapons locker.

Pulling out a silver and plastic-steel energy rifle, she closed the trunk with a loud, metal-rendering bang.

Good thing the vehicle was constructed of a ploy alloy impervious to both projectile attack and enraged FBI field agents.

Moving to the passenger side, she got in. When her door was down and secured, he hit the control stick and they lifted off. He keyed the instructions into the nav computer and pushed the throttle to maximum.

According to the ETA indicator on the dash they were twenty five minutes away, even at maximum velocity. From the corner of his eye he saw Angela already beginning to fidget impatiently.

Todd's heart ached. They'd been sitting there, eating burgers while Azelia Marks was flayed alive.

***

As they hovered over the log house, Todd studied the silent landscape. The house was dark and there were no signs of life. The alien shuttle was nowhere to be seen.

Todd had a sense of unease as he directed the air car to a landing spot about twenty meters from the front door. He'd already engaged the noise suppression system, which would hopefully mask their arrival.

There was a slightly bump in the quiet cockpit. Todd had wanted to turn on the radio during the trip, but Angela told him to stuff that idea in an uncomfortable place, so they rode in silence. The only sound was the air rushing past the cockpit windshield.

As soon as he'd killed the engine, Angela was out, her weapon at the ready in one hand, her scanner in the other.

Todd stepped out onto the damp Earth. It must have rained recently because their were puddles of water peppering the soft ground.

Not that it mattered, his once shiny shoes were a mess with all this racing around the country after a crazed killer. He raced to keep pace with Angela, covering the distance to the side of the house as fast as he was able. Once there, they pressed against the moss-covered interlocking logs making up the wall.

Though he didn't know for certain, he suspected Pie had told him the correct location. During their telepathic contact, Todd sensed the alien's were as incapable of lying as they were of murder. They had no concept of deception —what they did was omit information from their response. The challenge was asking the right questions to get the answers he needed.

Todd and Angela moved with their backs the damp wall until they reached the front door. It hung off its hinges at an angle as if it would fall any second, somehow clinging to its tenuous grip like a desperate man clinging to a cliff.

Angela nimbly moved to the opposite side of the doorframe, moving quickly so as to avoid being a target framed nicely for anyone inside. It was a gutsy move, considering Mike Sikes might be waiting for someone to cross in front of the door.

No shot came.

Todd found himself taking a deep breath in relief. Angela wasn't even breathing hard, and her focused expression revealed her grim determination.

As they'd done before, she gave him hand signals. She wanted him to go first this time. He shook his head. She cast him a look of disgust, her gaze drilling into him.

He hadn't played at being a soldier in so long he was unsure if the old reactions would kick in, even in this situation. He'd back her up and do everything possible to see she didn't get shot. But he wasn't ready to die just yet.

After nodding grimly, with three fingers of her right hand she counted down. As the last finger disappeared she crouched low and bolted inside. He took a deep breath and followed her in, sweeping his weapon across the interior. There was no movement beyond the perimeter.

He moved across the dusty wooden floor, past the piles of discarded, rotting paper and old rags to a trap door. Shifting her gun to her left hand Angela flicked on the searchlight she'd attached to the barrel to light up the room.

She was studying the screen of her handheld scanner. Gazing at the floor she stopped moving, seemingly frozen in place. She'd found something.

"DNA," she whispered pointing at the floor with the bright white light to create a spotlight in miniature. Todd nodded uneasily.

"Whose?" he asked.

"Not Mike or Azelia. The bodies were moved." Todd swallowed hard to clear his mouth of bile. Too many dead already.

As they moved across the floor dust stirred up by their boots drifted through the white light like a cloud of undulating poison gas on some war-torn battlefield.

Todd spotted the rusted metal handle for the trap door and motioned toward it. Angela moved forward and knelt down to grasp the handle while Todd aimed his rifle at the spot where the door would swing aside. She nodded her head to signal she was counting.

One, two three... She heaved the door aside. It slammed into the wood floor with a loud bang. A cloud of dust shot into the air. Todd's throat tightened when particles invaded his nostrils and mouth. He suppressed the urge to cough and blinked through the gray cloud at the dark chasm that was the access to the cellar. It was pitch black.

Angela, her rifle pointed in the gaping hole the beam of light cutting a swath through the murk. She moved forward slowly until the flashlight had pierced the darkness in the stairwell. No movement. There was only the sound of their breathing, though Todd would later swear he could hear his heart pounding in his chest.

Todd moved forward until he stood opposite Angela and wished he, too, had a light to allow him to see. If she went down without him, he was in trouble.

Without prompting he moved ahead of her, down the creaking wooden steps into the pitch blackness, his gun at the ready. The flashlight on her weapon created a searchlight effect, illuminating the areas where it touched.

At the bottom of the steps there was a red splash of color, mingled with the coffee-colored, dry dirt covering the floor. His heart leapt into his throat – there was a river of rust red blood pooled at the bottom of the stairs. The blood had dried to the consistency of pudding.

He moved along the river, his eyes on the floor following the trail in the white of the light, until his head bumped into something heavy and sticky. He stepped back and aimed in his rifle at the object. It looked like a side of beef, covered in blood and hung to drain after the slaughter.

His stomach heaved as he realized what was hanging from the ceiling wasn't beef. It was human — or at least what was left of a human. Under the mass of swollen red meat were two white rimmed eyes — human eyes — staring unseeing at him.

He dropped his rifle in the dirt and fell to his knees in the puddles of blood. This was the last straw. He emptied his stomach contents over and over until only sour, yellow bile filled his mouth.

Glancing up he saw Angela, her features twisted in rage, playing the light over Azelia's skinned, already bloating corpse.

Without a word, Angela left him alone in the suddenly dark room. He heard her heavy footsteps as she climbed the steps to the upper floor.

Standing on shaky legs, he felt his way back to the stairs, the light from above guiding him to the main floor without incident.

Azelia Marks was dead and there was nothing that would change that fact.

The question now was what to do about it. They were no closer to catching Mike Sikes than when they'd started this mad dash across the country.

TWENTY THREE

THE ROOM WAS DARK — too dark, and quiet — too quiet. Mike tried to lift his head, but couldn't. Next he tried to move an arm or a leg, but this, too, was unsuccessful. Someone had placed restraints around his arms and legs.

He was trapped. But his mind still worked. There was a pain in right arm where something had been inserted. They must have taken some blood. He frowned. Why?

His mind had always been his greatest asset. His mind had the most clarity when he killed. It had always been that way. When he was nine years old, he discovered killing the neighbor's prize winning cat had been easy. And it was fun to kill. Most people were too stupid to believe that anyone would commit vicious acts of torture and murder just for sport. Just because it was fun to watch suffering and death.

It thrilled him to watch other living things suffer. In his mind, he was powerful when he killed.

This clarity gave him the power to devise his escape plans. It hadn't worked in prison; but they didn't allow him to kill. Now that he had killed, his power had returned. No one, not even aliens, could hold Mike Sikes.

He smirked to himself in the darkness. They lied to him and the world. "How wonderful."

The sound of his own voice echoed around him.

Then he heard a whooshing sound and there was a sudden burst of white light that made him wince and squeeze his eyes shut.

Carefully he opened one eye to a rainbow of spots that danced across the white walls of the room. He realized he was lying on his back atop the most comfortable bed he'd ever been on. It seemed to fit the contours of his body as if it were constructed specifically for him.

In a manner of speaking… There was a voice inside his head. Welcome, Mr. Sikes. The Vel'Tan has brought you to our ship, currently orbiting your planet.

Mike heart sang. His reward. He would leave the Earth behind. His life's work was at last complete. He would new find fresh sources of pleasure in the stars on the aliens' home world.

No, I'm afraid not, Mr. Sikes. Your fragile frame would never survive the journey to our home. Humans are not sufficiently evolved for interstellar travel, yet.

Mike considered this for a moment. Then why was I brought here?

The Vel'Tan needs practice.

It occurred to Mike that he'd had been the perfect teacher. They were about to treat him to a unique experience. His eyes narrowed, then a slow smile crept across his pale face. They were going to kill him.

This might be fun. The alien voice did not respond.

He heard footsteps, then saw Pal's face leaning over him. That gentle, patient smile gazing at him with his red, emotionless eyes.

"I hope I do this right," said Pal.

"Oh, I'm sure you'll do fine," said Mike.

I wonder how long I'll last.

He felt the sting of the first cut of the razor-sharp blade into his flesh.

Funny how it hurts so much.

A trickle of the warm blood seeped from the wound created as the knife ran along his skin. His breathing remained level as Pal proceeded to methodically strip away his skin in asymmetrical, two inch strips.

He's good at this. Mike's mind surged with pride.

High praise from our teacher. We will be forever grateful; thank you, said the voice inside his head.

At least that bitch Cody won't get any satisfaction from my death. If she'd killed me, my death would've been as meaningless as if I'd died in the damned gas chamber. I've cheated them of their fun. I'm performing a public service.

There was sharp bite of the knife as another strip of flesh was cut away from his body.

Soon I'll be dead and free of this cursed universe. Maybe I'll ascend to heaven where I will be useful… no… more likely hell…to sit at my master's right hand…

Mike's mind began to wander and the room began to swirl and revolve like some bird's-eye view as he drifted in and out of consciousness. The glowing white walls seemed to pulsate with energy — moving in and out as if the ship itself were a living, breathing being.

The edges of his vision became darker as his mind slipped even further away. He closed his eyes to steady himself as death approached. The burning pain filled his mind with exquisite torture as it shot through his body, making his senses come alive.

He felt elation as the abyss gripped him and pulled him into a swirling vortex of darkness.

Fuck you, b—

***

Todd caught up with her at the air car. Angela sat in the passenger seat with the door swung open. Her eyes were filled with tears, and she sobbed as she tried to wipe the tears from her eyes as she repeatedly failed to dial a number into the cell phone.

"Fuck!" She flung the phone down on the seat next to her where it lay, face-up, the view screen glowing.

She buried her face in her hands as her body was wracked by deep sobs.

Todd stood watching this strong-willed woman in anguish. Was it her fault she was human? Of course not.

Finally her sobs ebbed and she lifted her head to stare at Todd through red-rimmed eyes. "I'm not supposed to get emotionally involved with victims…."

"I know," he said softly. FBI agents were supposed to remain impartial and somehow immune to the carnage around them. But, for God's sake they were only human beings not robots. Angela took this Mike thing personally — too personally.

Todd moved forward and rested one hand on her shoulder. She didn't make a move to stop him or rebuff his attempt to comfort her.

Suddenly his entire body jerked as an image invaded his mind. His hand dropped away from Angela's shoulder and his knees became weak and rubbery. He fell against the side of the air car holding his head with one hand. He winced and closed his eyes to stop the world from spinning out of control.

"What is it, Road?" Angela's brow wrinkled and her eyes narrowed.

"He's dead…"

"Who?" Now she sounded anxious.

"Mike…"

"What?"

"Mike is dead. The aliens skinned him alive. Just as he did to Azelia."

"I don't get it." Her voice suddenly contained a hard edge.

How could she not understand? She was in shock. The news of the demise of her greatest enemy mustn't have registered yet. She'd wanted him dead and her wish had been fulfilled. Somehow Todd knew it wouldn't be enough.

He closed his eyes and saw that the image of a mutilated, human-like shape covered in blood, lying on a table of some kind, his eyes wide and sightless as if gazing into the void. Those eyes would haunt him forever.

Just as poor Azelia's body in the cellar would also haunt his dreams for years to come. He shivered.

The air car's dashboard link suddenly began to chatter. The system was back online. Angela and Todd stared at the link unit set in the dash and then at each other. Then they heard a voice — a voice that was impossible yet unmistakable in its tone. "Angela?" said the deep male voice of Lenard Williams, back, it seemed, from oblivion.

Fingers trembling, Angela picked up the portable link unit from the holder on the dash next to the unit. She looked at Todd, her gaze uncertain. He nodded his agreement. Yes, he heard the voice, too, she wasn't imagining it.

She lifted the voice-activated unit to her lips. "Len?" she asked tentatively.

"Thank God, Angela. Yes, it's me. I was so worried..."

Tears welled in Angela's already swollen eyes and began to travel down her cheeks in rivulets of salty water. Todd reached for the unit and took it from her trembling hands. She smiled broadly and nodded at him. "Agent Williams, it's Todd Road. I'm with Angela,.."

"Road? What the hell's going on?"

Todd felt the urge to laugh out loud but suppressed it. When he spoke again he was unable to keep the joy he felt from his voice. "We're so glad you're alive. What about the others? Guy and the other staff from KZAP?"

"Yeah we're all here...we're at the Onyx building... at your station... where are you two...?"

"We're in Grantville..."

"What?"

"It's a long story. We'll explain when we get back.."

Angela grabbed the cell phone after yelping there once again was a signal turned it on and began pressing the numbers Todd suspected was for her father.

"Okay...I guess..." said Williams clearly perplexed.

Angela looked relieved on so many levels. A world class weight was just lifted from her shoulders.

"Hi. Dad..." her mouth formed a weak smile. "We're headed back to get you. Sikes is dead." Her voice went soft, as she added, "Yes, her as well." After a brief pause during which she just listened without speaking she cut the connection. Looking at Todd her mouth formed thin line but her eyes drooped at the corners.

"Dad says hi."

Todd nodded. He didn't feel like talking right now. Too much had happened, but at least the world was rid of the last serial killer.

Six Months Later

"Anymore contact... with them?" asked Milt Cody over the link set in Todd's desk at KZAP studios.

"No, nothing..." Todd sighed. Now that Mike's gone and over the aliens have left they don't seem to have anything more to say to me." He paused almost afraid to ask then said, "How is she?"

He heard Milt chuckle. "She's actually doing well. Why don't you call her? I'm sure she'd love to hear from you."

Todd glanced up to see Amy's young, pretty face smiling at him from behind her glass wall. She winked at him and gave him a thumb's-up sign. He waved at her as if he were swatting a fly.

He grinned and shrugged. "Yeah, Milt, I just might do that."

"Okay. Good talking to you, Todd. Keep in touch."

"Will do, see ya." Todd cut then connection.

"How long we got?" he said to Amy.

"Five minutes till the news is over."

He nodded. "Angela Cody," he said to the voice-activated link. Almost immediately he heard Angela's voice saying hello.

"Hum..." he felt tongue-tied like some school boy.

"I know it's you, Road. What do you want?" He could tell by her tone she was mocking him, a good sign.

"Angela... Ang... Agent Cody... I was wondering if you have any new information you might share with an old, broken-down, talk-radio host a few minutes of your valuable time?"

"You're not old."

He smiled briefly. When he talked to her he didn't feel old. And after all that they'd shared, she was now a good friend.

The death of Mike Sikes had lifted a world-shattering burden off her shoulders, and maybe now she'd get back to enjoying life.

Before the aliens left they thanked Todd for his help (a message he wisely kept to himself). They were headed home. The aliens were convinced their new-found evil would bring God to them.

At least humanity finally knew they weren't alone in the universe, even if the aliens were a little crazy from a human perspective.

The world was back to normal, so maybe Todd and Angela could do a little something normal together, like normal people.

"Dinner tonight?" he blurted suddenly.

"Why you old dog, I thought you'd never ask. Sure. See you at eight. I'll pick you up at the studio. I'd better drive. I've seen you behind the wheel."

He chuckled. "Okay then it's a date. See you then." He cut the link.

He glanced up at the on air light over the producer's window and watched it light up. It was time to get back to work.

About the Author

Russ Crossley writes romance under the name R.G. Hart, mystery/suspense under the name R.G. Crossley, and science fiction and fantasy under his own. This year there will be re-issues the romantic comedies, Bachelorette: Zombie Edition by Champagne Books, and Antique Virgin by 53rd Street Publishing, paranormal romantic comedy, Zomopolis, and a new western romance entitled, The Fire In Their Hearts co-authored with R.S. Meger. In addition the near future suspense novel, The Last Serial Killer by R.G. Crossley will be released soon.

He has sold several short stories that have appeared in anthologies from Pocket Books, St. Matins Press, at Smashwords, Amazon, and other e-retail sites.

With his wife, romance author R.S. Meger, he owns and operates a small press publishing company, 53rd Street Publishing. The company began in April 2011 and now has over one hundred e-book titles and two print titles, with more planned in 2012.

He is a member of SF Canada and the Greater Vancouver Chapter of Romance Writers of America. He is also an alumni of the Oregon Coast Professional Fiction Writers Master Class taught by award winning author/editors, Kristine Katherine Rusch and Dean Wesley Smith.

To find a complete listing of his work check out his website http://www.rghart.com, http://russstory.blogspot.com.Razor's blog can be found at http://razorandedge.blogspot.com

Other books by the Author

Titles as R.G. Crossley

Short Stories

Razor and Edge Mysteries
The Kidnapping of Billy Buttons
String of Pearls
Death by Clown
Beggin' For Murder
Ragged Ice
The Grand Central Mystery

Non-Series Mysteries
A Day Without Sunshine
Mirror Image
Dangerous Waters
Cape Disappointment
Boomerang
The Watcher of Wayburn Street
The Apprentice
Drip!
A Beautiful Friendship and The Parrot of Doom
Robine's Diary
The Christmas Club
Loose Ends
Skullduggery
Splatter Pattern

It Takes Two

Anthologies

The Adventures of Razor and Edge: Five Tales From The Quirky Detective Team

Novels

Death of A Hairdresser

A Bad Case of Loyalty

The Last Serial Killer

Titles as Russ Crossley

Novels

Attack of the Lushites

Short Stories

Countdown

Shoeless Moe

Round Up At The Burger Bar: The Story of Trixie Pug, Parts 1, 2, 3, 4, 5

Five Minutes

Blossom Queen, Barbarian

The Secret

The Family Line

End of the Flies

With Death You Get the Eggroll

The Penguin Sleeps With The Fishes

Only The Worthy

Hero For A Day

End of Empire

Strange Bedfellows

Big Business

A Perfect Crime

The Wise Guy and The Pirates

In Search of the Perfect Cup

T.I.N. Men

The Legend of G and the Dragonettes

The Incredible Mr. Fix-It

Lock Stock and Barrel

Divided Loyalties

Cave of Wonders

A Family Empire

Until We Meet Again

Dragon Rising

Presents Anthology Series

Five Tales of Urban Fantasy

Five Tales of Bizarre Detectives

Five Tales of Mystery and Suspense

Five Tales of Weird Fantasy

Spies, Detectives, & Heroes

Tales of Twisted Crime

Five Tales of The Unexpected

Tales From Space

10 by Russ Crossley

Round Up At The Burger Bar: The Story of Trixie Pug, Parts 1- 5

The Beginning

Worlds of Science Fiction and Fantasy

More Tales of Mystery and Suspense

Ladies of the Jolly Roger

Justice Served

Titles as R.G. Hart

Short Stories

Tikka's Big Day

"My Partner the Zombie" — Hungry For Your Love Anthology (St. Martin's Press)

Big Hairy Deal

One Red Shoe

A Bad Day in Lunden Texas

Hook Island

Grind Manor

Novels

Bachelorette: Zombie Edition (coming soon from Champagne Books)

Antique Virgin

The Fire In Their Hearts with R.S. Meger (coming soon)

Zomopolis (coming soon from 53rd Street Publishing)

www.ingramcontent.com/pod-product-compliance
Lightning Source LLC
Chambersburg PA
CBHW060925120626
46557CB00003B/876

* 9 7 8 0 9 8 7 6 7 0 1 0 6 *